"Some days_____of my life is b_____t with my folks on the farm. Those were good memories. I haven't been that happy again," Brody said. "But I hope that I will. One day."

"Me, too," Michelle murmured softly.

Amazing that this perfect stranger understood. That they had this in common. The knot of emotion swelled until her throat ached and her eyes burned. It was grieving, she knew, for the better times in her life. Pastor Bill had told her that the best was still ahead of her. To have faith.

Is that the way Brody felt? Did he look around at other people who were starting their lives together and see their happiness? Did he long to be part of that warm, loving world of family and commitment the way she did? Did he feel so lonely some nights it hurt to turn the lights out and hear the echoes in the room?

Maybe Pastor Bill was right. Maybe life was like a hymn with many verses, but the song's melody remained a familiar pattern. One that God had written for each person singularly. And maybe she was starting the second verse of hers....

Books by Jillian Hart

Love Inspired

Heaven Sent #143
**His Hometown Girl* #180
A Love Worth Waiting For #203
Heaven Knows #212
**The Sweetest Gift* #243
*Heart and Soul #251

*The McKaslin Clan

JILLIAN HART

makes her home in Washington State, where she has lived most of her life. When Jillian is not hard at work on her next story, she loves to read, go to lunch with her friends and spend quiet evenings with her family.

HEART AND SOUL

JILLIAN HART

Published by Steeple Hill Books™

Steeple Hill®

STEEPLE HILL BOOKS

RECYCLED PAPER

ISBN 0-373-87261-5

HEART AND SOUL

This edition published by arrangement with Steeple Hill Books.

www.SteepleHill.com

Printed in U.S.A.

And the most important piece of clothing
you must wear is love. Love is what
binds us together in perfect harmony.

—*Colossians* 3:14

Chapter One

Senior Special Agent In Charge Gabe Brody shucked off his motorcycle helmet, still straddling the idling Ducati M900. He waited on the graveled turnout along the country road while the cell phone connected. The hot Montana sun felt good, and so did the chance to rest. His first time on a motorcycle in years and his thighs and back muscles hurt immensely.

He prided himself on being the best agent in his division, but the truth was that the hours spent in the gym couldn't prepare a man for the rigors of a mission.

Even if that mission involved riding a powerful motorcycle in the middle of a summer afternoon with heaven spread out all around him. He breathed in the fresh air that was sweetened with the scent of seeding grass and wildflowers from the surrounding fields.

Not much different from the kind of place where he'd been as a boy. The countryside was peaceful and he didn't mind looking at it while he waited to be connected with his commander. Finally, he heard his direct supervisor bark out his usual gruff salutation.

"Agent Brody here, sir. I'm on assignment in Montana and good to go."

"Watch your back, agent." Captain Daggers was an old-time agent who believed in a job done right. And who'd seen too much in his years at the Bureau. "The Intel we've got says this McKaslin fellow is a wild card. We can't predict what he's gonna do. You keep your head low. I don't want to lose my best agent."

"Don't worry, sir. I'm cautious." He patted his revolver tucked in its holster against his left side and ended the call.

He was ready to make his move. His first objective was to make contact with McKaslin. Brody figured that with heaven on his side, he'd soon have enough evidence for a team to move in on an arrest warrant.

Please, Father, let this mission be a safe one, fast and clean. It was his last assignment for the Bureau. He wanted a textbook case, a solid evidentiary trail and an arrest without incident, as he was known for. He'd built the last ten years of his reputation on working hard and smart, and he wanted to leave the same way. Without a single blot on his record.

What could go wrong in paradise? Brody breathed in the fresh country air, once again taking in the

scenery that spread out before him in rich fertile rolling hills. The beauty of it was deceptive. As if in-
justice never happened here. As if criminal activity
could not exist where the wide ribbon of river sparkled a brilliant and perfect blue.

Mountains jabbed upward, rimming the broad val-
ley spread out before him. Larks sang, a few cottonwoods rustled lazily in the breeze and the hum of
tractors in a distant field sparked a memory of his
childhood.

He'd been a farm boy in the quiet hills of West
Virginia. A lonely childhood and a hardworking one,
and sometimes he missed it and his parents who had
passed on when he'd turned twelve. When his happy
country life had come to an abrupt end.

Enough of that. Brody shut off the sadness inside
with a shake of his head. He yanked on his helmet
and drew down his shades. What sense was there in
looking back?

Life was in the here and now, he'd learned that
the hard way. Now was the only thing that mattered.
He'd leave the worry over tomorrow to God, and
make the most of what he had today.

And today he needed to get rolling. His stomach
rumbled something fierce—he'd skipped lunch
again. A sign of too much on his mind.

He'd find a room, grab a bite, right after he made
a pass through the McKaslin property. Get a feel for
the lay of the land and what he'd be up against.

The swish of an approaching vehicle on the two-
lane road was a surprise. He'd been sitting on the

pullout of a dirt driveway for eight minutes—he checked his watch—and no one had passed by. Until now. Was it too much to hope that it was Mick McKaslin speeding along in his truck?

Brody took one look at the ten-year-old Ford Ranger that had seen better days judging by the crinkled front bumper, the rust spot in the center of the hood and the cracked windshield. Nope, he didn't recognize the vehicle from the workup in his file. It wasn't Mick's truck.

He waited until the vehicle whipped by before he revved the Ducati's sweet engine, released the clutch and cut out of the gravel with enough spin to spit rocks in his wake.

He hadn't been on a bike since the counterfeiting bike gang down in Palm Springs five long years ago, and he felt rusty. He needed to practice, put the bike through its paces. Dust off his motorcycle skills so that when he drove up and asked old man McKaslin for a chance at a job, his cover would be flawless.

No one would see one of the top agents in his field, but a drifter on a bike who, like so many others across America, was looking for temporary work.

With the wind on his face and the sun on his back, Brody lost himself in the power and speed of the machine.

He intended to make this last case his best job. No matter what he faced.

Was it wrong to love shoes so much? Behind the wheel of her little blue pickup, Michelle McKaslin considered the three shopping bags crammed beside her on the bench seat. It was officially summer, so she needed the right shoes. The styles this summer were *so* cute—strappy flats and sassy mules and the softest suedes a girl just couldn't say no to.

Even if her credit card was significantly maxed.

Well, nothing good came without sacrifice. It was a tough job, but someone had to sacrifice themselves for fashion, right?

Her cell chirped out the melodious strains of Pachebel's Canon in D. That was the song she'd picked out for her trip down the aisle—not that she was getting married any time soon, but a girl had to hope. Besides, how could she sit through two of her older sisters' weddings and not imagine one of her own?

She dug in her purse with one hand, keeping a good hold of the wheel because she'd already run into a fence post while she'd been searching for her phone and had the dent to prove it. She'd learned her lesson. She kept her eyes on the road and on her mirror. There was a motorcycle buzzing up behind her. A bright red one. She didn't recognize the motorcycle or the broad-shouldered man whose face was masked by a matching red helmet. He wasn't anyone she knew, and she knew everybody. That's what you got for growing up in a small farming town. It was just the way it worked.

So, who was this guy? Probably someone passing through. She saw it all the time—drifters, travelers, tourists, mostly tourists. This guy looked young and fit.

Hmm, it never hurt a girl to look. She found her phone, hit the button and held it to her ear. "Hey, Jenna, talk to me."

"I'm dying and my shift isn't close to being over." Jenna, her best friend since the first grade, sounded absolutely bored.

Of course she was. What other way was there to be? They were living in the middle of nowhere. In the middle of rural Montana where growing grass was *news*. Where exciting headlines like the current price of hay, wheat, soybeans and potatoes dominated the radio stations' airwaves and headlined the local paper.

Her life was so uneventful it was a miracle she didn't die of boredom. Her life was good and she was grateful, but a girl could use some excitement now and then.

"Check this." Michelle leaned forward just enough to keep the biker in her side-view mirror.

Of course, he was passing her because she always drove the speed limit; one, she couldn't afford a ticket and two, she felt guilty breaking the law. "There's this really cute guy. At least, I think he's cute. Kinda hard to tell with the helmet. He's passing on the straight stretch like right down from my driveway and—"

"He's not a gross scary guy, is he?" Jenna was never too sure about men she didn't know.

With good reason, true. "But this is a daydream,

Jen. We've got to make it good. He's got these broad shoulders, strong arms, like he's in command of his bike."

"In command of the road." Jenna sighed, picking up on the game they'd played since they were freshmen in high school. "He's a bounty hunter, wrongly accused. A good man, but hunted."

"That's an old TV show," Michelle reminded her, taking her attention completely off the road as the man and his bike swept past her window. She caught a good profile, a strong jaw and the sense of steady masculinity. "How about a spy on the run, disenchanted?"

"Or how about a star hockey player. A man of faith, a man of integrity, taking a trip across the country looking for that piece missing from his life."

"The love of his life," Michelle finished and they sighed together. It was a nice thought—

"Oh! No!" She saw the tan streak emerge from the tall grass along the side of the road. A deer and a fawn dashed onto the road and turned to stare at the oncoming bike and Michelle's truck.

The phone crashed to the seat as Michelle hit the brakes and turned into the skid with both hands trying to figure out who was going to move first—the biker or the deer—and which way everyone was going to go.

A little help, please, Father, she prayed as time slowed down like a movie running too slow. Her vision narrowed. Only the road in front of her mattered. The biker had turned too fast, hit his brakes too hard and was going down. One strong leg shot out trying to break his fall, but all he was doing was wiping out right in front of her.

She aimed for the deep irrigation ditch, crossing the double yellow, bracing herself for the impact she knew was coming. She put both feet on the brake and prayed. The deer and fawn skipped safely off the road and disappeared into the field of growing alfalfa.

The man and bike fell in a graceful and final arc to the pavement and skidded. She heard the crash of metal and the revving engine rise and then cut off. Her feet on the brake didn't seem to do any good. She was skidding toward the deep ditch and a solid wood telephone pole on the other side of it.

Then, as if angels had reached down to stop her, the truck's brakes caught and the vehicle jerked to a stop.

Silence.

Thank you, Lord. Michelle tumbled back against her seat, grateful that her seat harness had secured her tight. The truck's engine coughed and died. In the space between one breath and another she saw the man on the ground. He was as motionless as a rag doll sprawled on the two-lane county road.

She grabbed her phone only to hear Jenna sobbing. "Michelle? Can you hear me? Are you okay? I'm calling the police—"

"I need an ambulance," she said in a rush. "Not for me. The motorcycle guy. Tell them to hurry."

She ripped off her seat belt, leaped from the truck and flew across the road. Dropped to her knees at the fallen man's side.

He was so still. All six feet of him. His black leather bomber jacket was ripped at the shoulder where blood streamed through a tear in the seam of his black T-shirt. His chest rose and fell in shallow breaths.

Good. That meant he was alive. *Thank God.* She leaned over him, careful not to move him. ''Mister? Can you hear me?''

''Seraphim for the win'' came a muffled response from behind the shaded visor.

Seraphim? He was talking about angels? He *must* be at death's door. *Oh, please don't die on me, mister.*

''Mister, hold on. Help is coming.'' She lifted his visor with her fingertips. His eyes were closed, but those dark lashes were perfect half moons on the sun-browned perfection of his face. A proud nose, high cheekbones. No obvious signs of injury. ''Mister, do you know your name?''

His eyelashes flickered, giving her a glimpse of dark brown eyes before those thick black lashes swept downward.

Where was the fire department? Michelle glanced up and down the road. Empty. There was no one! Even the deer had fled the scene and there was only her to help him—like she knew what to do!

He clearly needed help. A big drop of blood oozed from beneath the left side of his helmet, over his left

brow. She yanked down the sleeve of her faded designer denim jacket that she'd gotten on sale for an
unbelievable one hundred and twenty dollars, and
wiped away the trickling blood. Was it a head injury? What if he was suffering from head trauma?
She was a faithful TV watcher of medical dramas,
but what did she know about intracranial hemor-
rhaging?

He moaned, still unconscious, and moved into her
touch as if he needed her comfort. Tenderness rolled
through her. She watched a shock of his dark hair
dance in the wind, brushing her knuckles. Her heart
tugged at the brief connection. He dragged in a
shaky sigh and his dark lashes fluttered again.

Please, Father, help him. He looked so vibrant
and strong, so fit and healthy, like a mighty dream
of a man who'd fallen to the ground before her.

Except his skin was warm and he moaned again.
He was no dream but a flesh-and-blood man.

She slid two fingers down the warm leather of his
jacket's collar to feel the steady pound of his pulse.
He was breathing. His heartbeat was strong.

"Hold on, mister."

His eyelashes fluttered again.

"Help is coming. I promise."

Who was speaking? Brody wondered as he struggled against the dark. He flashed back to scuba
school, when he'd been underwater without air,
training for every disaster, fighting off fake enemies
and holding his breath. The moment he'd been free,
his lungs had been close to bursting as he surged up,
up, up toward the glowing light. Once again fighting

with all his might, he broke through the light and opened his eyes.

''Why, welcome back.''

Her voice was light music, and his vision was nothing but brightness and a round blur of a shadow directly overhead. The bright light speared pain through his skull. Dimly he registered the pain but his body felt so far away.

Who was talking to him? It was that silhouette before his eyes. Wait, it was no silhouette but an angel kneeling over him, golden-haired and radiating light. A light so pure and perfect, he'd never seen the like.

Where was he? A fraction of a memory flashed into his mind. The rumbling vibration of the bike's engine, the kiss of the summer wind on his face, the rush of the asphalt beneath him as he shifted and the deer and fawn leaping onto the road in front of him.

He was dead. That's what happened. The crash had killed him and he was looking at heaven. At an angel who watched over him with all of the good Lord's grace.

Boy, his captain was sure going to be disappointed, and Brody was sad about that, but he'd never seen such beauty. It filled his soul, made insignificant the pain beginning to arch through his body—

Wait. He was in pain? That didn't seem right. And he was lying on something hard—the road. And where was St. Peter? No pearly gates, no judgment day.

Pain slammed against him like a sledgehammer drilling into his chest. He wheezed in a breath, alive, on earth and gazing up into the face of the most beautiful woman he'd ever seen.

"Lie still." Her voice was like the sweetest of hymns. Her touch was like a healing balm as she eased him back onto the ground.

He hadn't realized he'd even lifted his head, but he was breathless as he rested against the road. His senses cleared, and he could feel the breeze shivering over him, the heat radiating off the pavement. See the blue of the flawless sky and the peaches-and-cream complexion of the concerned woman gazing intently down at him.

"The paramedics are coming." Relief shone in her deep blue eyes. "You just lie still and have faith. You're going to be fine."

She said those words with such force that he believed her. Even with the pain rocketing through his head and jabbing through his ribs and zipping all the way down his right leg. He knew he was going to be fine.

The siren shrilled louder, closer, magnifying the pain in his throbbing head. He gritted his teeth, refusing to give in to the inviting darkness of unconsciousness. He *could* hold on. He *would*.

She laid her hand against his unshaven jaw, and it was as if light filled him from head to toe.

Who *was* she? Why did she affect him this way? Maybe it was shock setting in or how hard his head had hit the pavement, but when he looked at her, his soul stirred.

Boots pounded to a stop. Men dropped equipment and a uniformed man—a local fireman—dropped to his knees.

"Had a spill, did you?" Kindness and wisdom were written into the lines on the man's face. "No, don't try to sit up. Not yet. What's your name, cowboy?"

"Brody," he said before the fog cleared from his brain and he realized he was in big trouble.

He'd blown his cover. He hadn't been on the job more than five minutes, and what did he do?

Blow it all to bits. He'd given his real name instead of the cover name he'd been given. And this was his final mission. When he wanted to go out with a bang, not hanging his head.

It's not over yet, he realized, biting his tongue before he could say his first name. He had to think quick.

"Brody," he repeated. "Brody Gabriel."

It wasn't the name that matched his false ID and social security card, his insurance information and the registration papers to the bike, but he'd worry about that later.

This mission could still be salvaged.

"Don't worry about your bike," the fireman reassured him, the name Jason was embroidered in red thread on his shirt, "It's still in one piece. Sure is a beauty. How'd you wipe out on a straight stretch?"

"A deer."

"Rough, man." The fireman shook his head and patched in his equipment.

Brody tried looking around again. Where had his rescuer gone? All he knew was that he couldn't see her. He tried to sit up and nausea rolled through him. He sank weakly to the pavement and let the medics check his pulse and blood pressure.

While they did, he took a quick inventory of his pain. His ribs were killing him. But his right ankle hurt worse.

Lord, Brody prayed, *please don't let my leg be broken.* That would be an end to everything. He'd worked hard to prepare for this mission. No one was as primed and prepared as he was. He refused to hand over his hard work to a junior agent. This was supposed to be the mission he'd be remembered for.

"I'm good," he told Jason. "I just need to sit up, get my bearings. I hit pretty hard going down."

"You've got a mild concussion to prove it, is my bet." The fireman flicked a flashlight and shone it into Brody's eyes. "Let us take care of you. Sometimes you can't tell how bad you're hurt right off. It's good to go to the hospital, let 'em take their pictures and run their tests. Make sure you're A-OK. Now move your fingers for me. Can you feel that?"

"Yep." Brody's relief was tempered by the cervical collar they snapped around his neck. His toes moved, too. Another good sign.

That's when she moved into his line of sight. His golden haired rescuer leaned against the front quarter panel of the sheriff's cruiser and crossed her long legs at the ankles.

My, but she was fine. Tall, slim and pure goodness. Her long blond hair shimmered in the sun and danced in the breeze. Her blue eyes were now hidden behind sunglasses, but her rosebud mouth was drawn into a severe frown as she gestured toward the road, as if describing what had happened.

She wore a faded denim jacket over a light pink shirt and stylish jeans. The sleeves were rolled up to reveal the glint of a gold watch on one wrist and a glitter of a gold bracelet on the other. Her voice rose and fell and he was too far away to pick up on her words, but the sound soothed him. Made longing flicker to life in the middle of his chest.

He'd never felt such a zing of awareness over a woman before. He was on duty. He was the youngest senior agent for the Federal Bureau of Investigation. He knew better than to take a personal interest in anyone when he was dedicated to a case, to upholding the laws of this great land.

What he ought to do was put her out of his mind, ignore the sting of longing in his chest and concentrate on his job.

Then she turned in profile to gesture toward the side of the road, and that's when he recognized her. The perfect slope of a nose, the delicate cut of cheekbone and chin. She was one of the McKaslin girls. Michelle.

The youngest daughter of the family he'd come to investigate.

Chapter Two

In the harsh fluorescent lights of Bozeman General's waiting room, Michelle stared down at her new toe-thong, wedge sandals that went so perfectly with her favorite bootleg jeans.

It was a perfect sandal. And on sale, too. She'd been wanting a pair of wedge sandals for over two months now, salivating each and every time she saw a model wearing them on the pages of her beloved magazines. So, when she'd saw them in the window display at the mall on her way to the Christian bookstore, she'd bought them on impulse.

An hour ago, she'd felt rad. Better than she'd been in a long time. Tapping across the parking lot to her truck with her shopping bags had given her great satisfaction. As if all her problems in life were solved with six pairs of new shoes.

Until she'd seen the medics working on the motorcycle guy, their faces grim. Their equipment had reflected the sun's harsh rays in ruthless stabs of light that had hurt her eyes and cut straight to her soul.

She could still see that man wipe out right in front of her. The drag of his body on the pavement, the ricochet of his head hitting the blacktop, the deathly stillness after his big body had skidded to a stop.

She shivered, horrified all over again. It was by God's grace he'd opened his eyes, she decided. A miracle that he'd survived. She'd never realized before how fragile a human life could be. Flesh and bone meeting concrete and steel…well, she hated to think of all that could have happened.

Or all the catastrophic ways the man the firemen called Brody could still be hurt.

"Go on home," Sheriff Cameron Durango had told her at the scene.

Go home? She hadn't caused the accident, but she felt responsible. She couldn't explain why. She just was. From the moment she saw his big male form sprawled out on the road, the rise and fall of his chest, the ripple of the wind stirring the flaps of his jacket, she'd been involved.

When she'd lifted his visor and saw the hard cut of his high cheekbones, the straight blade of his nose and the tight line of his strong mouth, he looked strong and vulnerable at the same moment.

She'd *seen* him crash. She'd seen him bleed. She couldn't just walk away as if it hadn't happened. As if she didn't care. As if she didn't have a heart. She couldn't have left a wounded bird in the road, let alone a wounded man. Even if she'd been waiting for hours and hours.

Where was he? What was taking so long? Okay, the waiting room was crammed with people coughing and sneezing and one man was holding a cloth to his cut hand—the nurse came out and took him away quickly. They were busy, she got that, but what about Brody? Was he so hurt that he was in surgery or something scary like that? Maybe she ought to go up to the desk and ask.

She grabbed her purse and tucked her cell safely inside. With great relish, she abandoned the hard black plastic chair that was making her back ache. She wove around sick people and some cowboy's big-booted feet that were sticking way out into the aisle.

The line behind the check-in window was long. She fell into place. But when she looked up, she nearly fell off her wedge-sandals at the sight of Brody limping down the wide hallway toward her.

Alive. Walking on his own steam. He looked bruised but strong, and her spirit lifted at the sight. Relief left her trembling and weak, and wasn't that really weird because he was like a total stranger?

He was holding his helmet in his left hand and a slip of paper in the right. The white slash of a bandage over his left brow was a shocking contrast to his brown hair and sun-golden skin.

His eyes were dark, shadowed with pain and his mouth a tight unhappy line as he strolled up to her. "I remember you."

He could have said that with more enthusiasm. Like with a low dip to his voice, the way a movie star did when he was zeroing in on his ladylove for the first time. He'd say, with perfect warmth in the words, "I remember you," and the heroine would flutter and fall instantly in love.

Yeah, that would be better than the way Brody said it, as if she were a bad luck charm he wanted to avoid. "They're letting you walk out of here, so that must mean you're all right."

"My ankle's wrapped. I've got a few stitches and I'm as good as new."

"I'm glad. I mean, like, you really crashed hard. I couldn't go home until I knew for sure that you were all right."

So, *that's* what she was doing here.

Brody stuffed the pain prescription in his pocket and mulled that little piece of information over. According to his research, Michelle McKaslin was the spoiled favorite of the family, the youngest of six girls. The oldest had been killed in a plane crash years ago. She was working two jobs, one at the local hair salon and the other at her sister's coffee shop, and still living at home. The Intel he had on her was that she loved to shop, talk on the phone with her friends and ride her horse.

"You came here to see a doc, too," he said, not believing her. Nobody sat in a waiting room for hours without a good reason. Unless she suspected who he was. What had he muttered before he'd come to? Had he given himself away? "I saw your truck skid to a stop. Hit your head on the windshield, didn't you?''

Her big blue eyes grew wider. ''Oh, no, I was wearing my seat belt. It just looked so scary with the way they put the neck collar on you and took you off in the ambulance. I can't help feeling responsible, you know, since I was there. I'm really glad you're not seriously hurt. I started praying the minute I saw the deer leap onto the road.''

There wasn't a flicker of dishonesty in her face. Only honest concern shone in her eyes, and her body language reinforced it. None of the paperwork he had on her had indicated she'd be sincere. That surprised him. He didn't run into nice people in his line of work.

Unless the niceness was only a mask, hiding something much worse inside.

''Let me get this straight. You drove all the way back to the city to sit in a waiting room for two hours just so you knew I was all right?''

''Yep. This is Montana. We don't abandon injured strangers on the road.''

She seemed proud of that, and he had no choice but to take what she said as the truth. He relaxed, but only a fraction.

''Wait one minute!'' the clerk behind the desk shouted at him, forcing him to abandon Michelle and approach the window where intimidating paperwork was pushed at him. ''Your insurance isn't valid.''

''Not valid?'' It figured. None of his ID matched his new name. His cover was supposed to be Brad

Donaldson, and that's what his Virginia driver's license said, his new insurance card, everything.

"We can make arrangements if you can't pay the entire bill right now." The woman with the big, black rim glasses and the KGB frown could have had a job at the Bureau intimidating difficult people.

Brody glanced at the total. Blinked. His heart rate skyrocketed. "Are you sure you billed me right? I didn't have a liver transplant."

The woman behind the window turned as cold as a glacier. "Our prices are so high because of people who do not pay their hospital bills."

Great. Why did that make him feel like dirt? He paid his bills. Not that he had eight hundred dollars in his wallet to spare.

The woman, whose badge identified her as Mo, lifted one questioning brow. She glanced at his biker's scarred bomber jacket, the right shoulder seam torn, and the unshaven jaw as if drawing her own conclusions.

Michelle stepped discreetly away from the scene to give Brody his privacy. She probably should go home now that she knew he was all right and could go on his way. She'd tell him where his bike was, and hand over his bike's saddle pack. Yep, that would be the sensible thing to do.

"Are you able to pay the bill in full?" Mo demanded.

"Yes, but I need an ATM machine."

"Do we look like a bank?"

The big man sighed in exasperation as he rubbed his brow. His head had to be hurting him.

Just walk away, Michelle. That's what her mom would say. *Sure, he looks nice and he's handsome, but he's still a stranger.*

A stranger stranded in a city without his own transportation, she remembered. The sheriff had called the local towing company to have the bike hauled away.

What should she do? Maybe the angels could give her a sign, let her know if this man was as safe as she thought he was. He didn't fit the stereotype of a biker, if there was one. He was youngish, probably in his late twenties. He wore a plain black T-shirt and a pair of Levi's jeans. But it was his boots that made her wonder.

They were special order, handmade and cost more than she made in three months. Not just anyone could afford those boots to ride a motorcycle. Just who was this handsome stranger? Maybe he was a software designer on a vacation. Or a vice president of a financial company getting away from the city on an always-longed-for road trip.

There she was, off on her romantic daydreams again. The question was, did she help him or not?

As Brody leaned forward to thumb through the contents of his wallet, a gold chain eased out from beneath the collar of his T-shirt. A masculine gold cross, small but distinctive, dangled at the curve of the chain.

He was a man of faith. It was all the sign she needed. Michelle stepped forward, intending to help.

"Are you going to pay or not?" Mo demanded.

"I'll give you what's in my wallet, how's that?" One-hundred-dollar bill after another landed on the counter.

He had that much cash? Michelle's jaw dropped. Didn't he have credit cards? It was a travesty. "I'll take you to the bank, if you need a ride."

Brody shoved the pile of bills at the somewhat mollified Mo and pivoted on the heels of his boots. His dark eyes surveyed her from head to her painted toenails. "You'd help me out, just like that?"

"Sure. I don't think you're dangerous and you *are* in need. I don't think you should walk very far being hurt like that." She reached into her purse and started rummaging around. Where had her phone gone to? She pushed aside her sunglasses and kept digging. "Oh, here it is. Is there someone you should call? To let them know you're okay?"

He stared at the cell phone she offered him. "No, thanks. I've got my own phone. Besides, there's no one waiting for me."

"*Someone* has to be concerned about you. A mother? A wife?" Since he wasn't wearing a gold band, it didn't hurt to ask. "A girlfriend?"

He blushed a little and stared at the ground. "No, there's no girlfriend."

"There used to be one?" Okay, call her curious. But she had to know. Maybe he'd had his heart broken. No, wait, maybe he'd been jilted at the altar, and he'd taken off on his bike not knowing where he was headed only that he had to get away and try to lose the pain.

The shadows in his eyes told her that she was close. The poor man. Anyone could see how kind he was. How noble. It was in the way he stood— straight and strong and in control of himself. A real man.

She sighed as she stuffed her phone back into her purse. "Which bank do you need to go to?"

"I don't care. Nearest cash machine is good enough." Brody crumpled his receipt and jammed it in his coat pocket.

"No problem. Do you want to get your prescription filled, too?"

"No. Where's my bike? My pack?"

"The town mechanic towed your bike to his shop in town, but I thought to grab your bag. I told the sheriff I'd look after you. Since I feel responsible."

"It wasn't your fault."

"I know, but I was there. I saw you fall. I've got to know that you're all right." She had the energy and grace of a young filly, all long-legged elegance as she led the way toward the electronic doors. "You've got to be hungry, too. And you'll need a place to stay. Unless you have reservations nearby?"

Things couldn't be working out better if he'd planned it this way. What seemed like a disaster was a godsend. How many times had that happened in his missions over the years? Brody knew, beyond a doubt, that's what happened when a person followed his calling. The Lord found a way to make everything work out for the good.

Brody decided to ax his plans and improvise. Go with the flow. "No, I don't have a place to stay."

"Then we'll find you something."

Excellent. He couldn't ask for more. He didn't mention the local classifieds he'd pored through on the Internet at his office in Virginia. Or the fact that he'd already chosen a place to stay in town not far from the McKaslin ranch. A dirt-cheap hotel with convenient kitchenettes that rented by the week. What a biker like him would be expected to afford.

What would Michelle McKaslin suggest? This opportunity was too good to turn down and adrenaline pumped through his blood. He forgot that he was hurt. That pain was shrieking through his ankle and up his leg. With Michelle McKaslin willing to help him, it could only help his mission.

He fell in stride beside her, only to have her dart away from him in a leggy, easy sprint. Where was she going?

"Oh, I'll be right back," she called over her shoulder. She trotted down the brightly lit sidewalk in front of the emergency area.

Away from him. What was going on?

He watched Michelle dash up to a gray-haired, frail woman. The two spoke for a moment. The elderly woman dressed neatly in a gray pantsuit and a fine black overcoat looked greatly relieved.

Someone she knew? Brody wondered. From his records he'd already ascertained that Michelle had a grandmother. But the woman Michelle was speaking to didn't look anything like Helen, whose picture he'd seen in the local paper as a member of the Ladies' Aid.

To his surprise, Michelle escorted the older woman toward him and pointed to the wide doors to the desk where Mo was now collecting information from another patient. "Right there, she can help you," Michelle said.

"Oh, you are a good girl. Thank you so much." Looking seriously grateful, the older woman made her way to Mo's counter.

"She was lost. It *is* confusing around here," Michelle said easily as she hopped off the sidewalk onto the pavement. "They need more signs."

Brody was speechless. Michelle really *was* a sweetheart. She'd stopped to help an elderly woman find her way with the same good spirit as she was helping him tonight. Unbelievable. Yet, true. He didn't see that often in his line of work.

He recognized the somewhat rusty and slightly dented 1992 Ford Ranger as the same one he'd been passing this afternoon. Dust clung to the blue side panels and someone had written "wash me" on the passenger door.

"That was probably one of my sisters," Michelle commented as she unlocked the door for him. "When I find out which one, she will regret it."

Michelle looked about as dangerous as a baby bunny. Still, he recognized and appreciated her sense of humor. "A cruel retribution?"

"At the Monopoly board, of course. We play board games every Sunday night. Fridays, when we can manage it."

"How many sisters do you have?" Although he already knew the answer.

"I have four older sisters." She didn't mention the oldest sister, although she sounded sad as she walked around the back of the truck to the driver's side. "They are great women, my sisters. I love them dearly. They are so perfect and beautiful and smart. And then there's me."

He settled in on the bench seat. "What's wrong with you?"

"What isn't?" She rolled her eyes, apparently good-natured about her shortcomings and dropped into place behind the steering wheel. "First of all, I didn't go to college. Disappointed my parents, but I've never liked school. I got good grades, I worked hard, but I didn't like it. I like working with hair."

Michelle yanked the door shut with an earsplitting bang. "I like my job at the Snip & Style. I'm fairly new at it, and it takes years to build a clientele, but I'm doing pretty well."

"You're a beautician?"

"Yep." The engine turned over with a tired groan. "What do you do?"

"I used to ride rodeo," he lied, and his conscience winced.

It was his job, and being dishonest had never bothered him like this before. He'd justified it all knowing it was for the greater good. He was trying to bring justice, right wrongs, catch bad guys.

As he gazed into Michelle's big blue eyes, where a good brightness shone, he felt dirty and ashamed.

"Rodeo? Oh, cool. I used to barrel race. I was junior state champion two years in a row. I'm not as good as my sister, though. Her old room at home has one whole wall full of her ribbons."

"You have a horse?"

"Yep. Keno. I ride him every day. I've been riding since I was two years old."

"I was eighteen months." Brody couldn't believe it. Not everyone he met had been riding nearly as long as they could talk. "My dad was a cattleman. He'd take me out in the fields with him as early as I could remember. I'd spend all day in the saddle on my pony, Max. I rode better than I could walk."

"Me, too. All my sisters had horses, and so I *had* to ride, too. My mom has pictures of me sitting on my sister's horse, Star, when I was still a baby. I got my own pony for my fifth birthday."

"I traded in my pony for an American quarter horse. My dad and I would pack up after a day in the fields and head up into the mountains. We'd follow trails up into the wilderness, find a good spot and camp for the night. Just like the mountain men used to do. Those were good times."

"I know what you mean. Before my oldest sister died, my family used to take trips up into the mountains. We'd ride up into the foothills and we'd spend a few days up there. Catching trout and having the

best time. Real family times. We don't do that anymore.''

Sadness filled her, and Michelle stopped her heart
because it hurt too much to think about how the
seasons of a person's life changed. It wasn't fair. She
missed the closeness of her family. It seemed like
everything she'd ever known was different. Her sisters had moved out on their own. Karen and Kirby
had gotten married. Michelle couldn't believe it. She
was an aunt now.

''That's what I like about taking off on my motorcycle.''

''Camping?''

''Yep. That's what I've been doing, but not tonight.'' Brody's rumbling baritone dipped self-
consciously. As if he were embarrassed he'd wiped
out.

No wonder. It took a tough man, one of determination and steel and skill, to survive on the rodeo
circuit. One who wouldn't like to be seen crashing
his motorcycle, even if it was practically unavoidable. ''You're probably a little sore from hitting the
pavement so hard.''

''That's an understatement.'' His grin was lopsided, and the reflection of the dash lights made him
impossibly handsome. ''It sounds as if you miss going camping.''

''Not so much. I'm sorta fond of hot water and
plumbing.'' It was hard to talk past the painful emotion knotted in the center of her chest. ''I guess what
I miss is the way things used to be. How close we

all used to be. The fun we used to have. I know everyone grows up and everything changes, but it just seems sad.''

"Some days I think the best part of my life is behind me. Times spent with my folks on the farm. Those were good memories. I haven't been that happy again."

"I hope that I will. One day."

"Me, too."

Amazing that this perfect stranger understood. That they had this in common. The knot of emotion swelled until her throat ached and her eyes burned. It was grieving, she knew, for the better times in her life. Pastor Bill had told her that the best was still ahead of her. To have faith.

Is that the way Brody felt? Did he look around at other people who were starting marriages and families or raising their children and see their happiness? Did he long to be part of that warm loving world of family and commitment the way she did? Did he feel so lonely some nights it hurt to turn the lights out and hear the echoes in the room?

Maybe Pastor Bill was right. Maybe life was like a hymn with many verses, but the song's melody remained a familiar pattern. One that God had written for each person singularly. And maybe she was starting the second verse of hers.

She had faith. She had no patience, but she had faith. And knowing that a perfect stranger, and one as handsome as the man beside her, was walking a similar path helped.

She pulled up to the well-lit ATM at the local bank and put the truck in Park. As Brody ambled up to the machine, rain began to fall. Small, warm drops polka-dotted her windshield and felt like tears.

Chapter Three

The plump woman behind the motel's front desk cracked her gum and tilted her head to the side, forcing her bleached beehive at an angle that reminded Michelle of the Leaning Tower of Pisa. "Honey, we're booked up solid. It's tourist season. There are no vacancies from here to Yellowstone, but I'll call around for you, if you'd like. See if there was a last-minute cancellation somewhere."

"I'd sure appreciate that, ma'am." Brody sounded patient and polite.

Michelle noticed he was looking pasty in the bad overhead lighting. He was in pain, she realized with a cinch in the middle of her chest. Much more than he was letting on. She remembered the prescription he didn't want to fill.

So, he was a tough guy, was he? She wasn't surprised.

But she was shocked at the dark patches in the

woman's hair. Someone had done a bad job—a seriously sloppy coloring job. Shameful, that's what it was.

That was something she could fix. Michelle dug around in her purse and found a business card. This side of Bozeman wasn't far at all from the pleasant little town she lived and worked in, and so, why not?

God had given her a talent for hairstyling, and maybe she ought to do good where she could. She dug around for a pen, found one beneath her compact and wrote on the back of her card, "Free cut and coloring. Just give me a call."

"Maybe you'd better sit down before you fall down." Michelle eyed Brody warily. He stood militarily straight, but dark bruises underscored his eyes. The muscles along his jaw were rigid, as if it took all his will to remain standing.

"I'm fine." His terse reply was answer enough.

Yep, definitely a tough guy. Too macho for his own good. Michelle rolled her eyes and capped her pen. He wasn't her responsibility, not entirely, but what was she going to do? Just leave him? He obviously needed help and he didn't even know it.

"I'm sorry," the clerk returned. "I've called all the chains and independents around. The closest vacancy I could find was a room in Butte."

An hour away. Brody groaned. That wasn't going to work. Maybe he'd call his emergency contact at the local office. See if he couldn't crash on a fellow agent's couch for the night. Brody thanked the woman for her trouble.

"If you're interested," Michelle said as she handed something to the woman. "On the house. For your trouble tonight."

"Why, that's awful nice of you." She beamed at Michelle. "I'll sure do that. I've been needing to make an appointment, and gosh, just couldn't fit it into my budget."

"Then I'll be seeing you." Michelle joined him at the door.

Had she just given away a free haircut? Brody pondered that.

"What are we going to do with you, mister?" Rain dripped off the overhead entrance and whispered in the evening around them as she flipped through her key ring.

"Abandon me in the street?" He shrugged. "I'll be fine. Let me get my pack out of your truck before you go."

"I'm not leaving you here." With a flick of her hair, she marched toward her truck, fearless in the rain. "What are you standing there for? Hurry up. You're coming with me."

"As in, going home with you?"

"Isn't that what I said?"

No way. That was too good to be true.

"What are you going to do? Sleep in the rain? My parents have this big house. They won't mind a guest for the night."

An invitation to spend the night in the McKaslins' home. He was speechless at this rare opportunity.

"They'd take a stranger into their house, just like that?"

"You can have the bed over the garage. Don't worry. It's nice. You can get a good night's sleep, and in the morning one of us will drive you to town so you can check out the damage to your bike." With a shrug, Michelle unlocked her truck and climbed behind the wheel.

He swiped rain out of his eyes and took refuge inside the cab. Unbelievable.

As the rain began falling in earnest, tapping like a hundred impatient drummers on the roof, he had this strange, sinking feeling. Just like the time when he'd been diving and his gear hung up on a snag, pulling him down against his will. "You shouldn't be offering perfect strangers rides in your truck. Or to stay overnight in your parents' house."

"I trust you."

"You shouldn't."

"You're a man of faith." She touched her own dainty cross.

"I don't suppose you realize some people pretend to be what they're not. To take advantage of others." When he did so, he did it for justice. To protect the innocent citizens of this country.

He knew for a fact there were bad people in this world. And those bad people kept him and his colleagues well employed. Didn't she have a clue? "I *could* be dangerous."

"But you're not. I have a sense about these things." Michelle's smile was pure sunlight—gentle and bright and true—as she turned her attention to her driving.

Unaware that she was about to bring a wolf in sheep's clothes into her family's home. A protective wolf, but one just the same.

The hard edge of his trusty revolver cut into his side, mocking him, concealed in the slim leather holder beneath his leather jacket.

"Besides, what else are you going to do? Walk all the way to Butte? You're injured and I told you, I feel responsible."

The way Michelle saw it, God might have placed her on that road at that exact moment just so that Brody wouldn't be alone when he crashed to avoid the deer and her fawn.

Maybe she was *meant* to help him. As a Christian, it was her duty. How could she *not* help? It would be wrong.

She didn't know if her mom would see it that way, but she was absolutely sure that her dad would, because he was cool. By now, her parents ought to be used to her habit of bringing home strays, right?

Even if she'd never brought home a stray this big before.

Or one so handsome he made her teeth ache.

The house was dark, except for the lone lamp in the entryway. It wasn't Mom's Bible-study night. Or Dad's grange hall meeting night. Where were they? And didn't they know she worried?

Maybe they'd gone out to dinner. Could it be?

Afraid to hope, afraid to say it out loud, Michelle grabbed fresh linens from the hall closet. If her parents had gone out together, it would be the first time in six years. Ooh, the curiosity was killing her as she stole a pillow off Kendra's bed along with the plain blue comforter.

Brody. He'd turned down her invitation to come into the house and was checking out the apartment over the garage.

He sure was a courteous guy. Concerned about her safety. Maybe it came from the kind of life he'd lived. Always on the road with the rodeo. He'd probably seen a lot that she couldn't even dream of.

She liked that about him. That he was worldly. Experienced. But when he smiled, his eyes sparkled with a quiet kindness. She liked that. Which was too bad. Brody didn't have plans to stay. He was just passing through.

At least it didn't hurt a girl to dream.

She caught sight of him through the second-story windows. He stood gazing around the small apartment, wandering around to look at this or that. A zip of warmth flooded her heart, and she couldn't stop the sigh that bubbled up until she felt as if she were floating with it.

What a man. He stood like a soldier, alert, strong and disciplined, and so inherently good, it made her eyes glisten. She knew beyond a doubt that helping him was the right thing to do.

She closed the front door, skipped down the steps and dashed through the remaining splashes of the rainstorm. In no time at all she was bouncing up the steps and into the attic apartment where Brody turned to her.

And made her pulse stop.

"This is a nice place you've got here." Brody gestured around at the shadowed front room that led into the small kitchen.

But Michelle didn't bother to look around the place and admire it with him. How could she notice anything when he was so near? He'd taken his leather jacket off and folded it on the tabletop, leaving him in the black T-shirt where torn fabric gaped over another thick bandage.

Was her heart ever going to start beating again, she wondered as air rushed into her lungs and she could breathe. Maybe she'd waited too long to eat dinner—they'd grabbed takeout on the way out of Bozeman—and that's why she felt funny.

"Does someone live here?" Brody strolled to the wide front windows and closed the blinds. "Or do you just keep this place for random strangers in need of a good night's sleep and patching up?"

"The foreman used to live here until my dad had a cottage built down by the creek. Then my sister Karen lived here for a long time, but then she got married, and my uncle lost both his job and his wife and needed some place to stay but he said it was too small…." Oh my, was she rambling? Yes, she definitely was. Stop it, Michelle.

"As it turns out, we don't have a foreman anymore, so my uncle took over the cottage last month.

So, no one's staying here right now." Was she still holding the sheets and stuff?

Yes. What was with her anyway, staring at handsome Brody as if she'd lost her cerebral cortex? She dropped the pillow, sheets and comforter on the corner of the couch.

She still felt nervous. Why suddenly now? Because she was alone with him, and that didn't make any sense at all. They'd been all alone in the truck. This felt different. When was the last time she'd been alone with a guy like Brody? Had she *ever*?

"I appreciate the hospitality." He favored his injured right ankle as he ambled over to grab the set of floral-printed linens. "I can't say that I've slept on pink and blue flowers before."

"Flowered sheets are more restful."

"Is that a scientifically proven fact?"

"Absolutely."

They should have been teasing, but it was something else. Something that flickered in an odd way in her chest. A warmth of emotion that she didn't know how to describe because she'd never felt it before.

She turned away. Feeling like this couldn't be a good thing. Vulnerable, that's what she was, and she didn't like it. She retreated to the open entry where a dark slash of the deepening night welcomed her. "The bedroom's through those doors. If you need anything, let me know."

"Thanks, Michelle. You don't know how much I

appreciate this.'' He looked sincere. Strong. Like everything a good man ought to be.

Michelle fled onto the tiny porch, pulling the door closed behind her. She felt her face flaming and her pulse jackhammering. She was feeling a strange tug of emotion, longing and admiration all rolled into one.

Great. Had he noticed?

Probably. How could he not? At least he was leaving come morning. She could pretend she didn't think he was the coolest man ever for a few more hours.

It wasn't like she had a chance with him. He was too worldly, and he had a life. It wasn't as if he was going to drop everything and move to a tiny town in Montana that was a pinpoint on a detailed state map.

Be real, Michelle.

Common sense didn't stop the stab of longing that pierced through her chest. It didn't stop the pain of it.

She wiped her feet on the welcome mat on the front porch. She locked the door behind her. As she did every night, she hung her denim jacket on one of the hangers inside the entry closet. There was a note tacked to the message board in the kitchen by the phone. Her mom was the queen of organization.

''Michelle, went to supper and a show with your gramma. Make sure you start the dishwasher when you get in. Don't stay up too late.''

There went the hope that her parents were out

together. After all this time, she knew better than to hope. But it was one of those wishes that never died, that flickered to life new and fragile every day.

The message light on the answering machine was blinking and she hit the playback button. The old machine ground and hissed and clicked. There was a message from older sister Karen, calling to remind Michelle about her shift tomorrow at the coffee shop. A message from some old guy looking for Dad.

Michelle groaned at the third message. It was from Bart Holmes. The farmer who lived down the road. The same Bart who'd been mooning after her sister Kirby, until Kirby had married.

As if! In disgust, Michelle erased Bart's nasal voice. She was *so* not interested in going out to dinner. She'd do her best to avoid him in church. She was not interested in joining his Bible study, either, thank you very much! Couldn't he get a clue?

Just her luck. The guys she didn't want to notice her, pursued her. And the one that she *did* want to notice her was so far out of her league, she might as well be trying to jump to the moon.

Give it up, Michelle. She squeezed dishwashing soap into the compartment and turned on the contraption. She left the kitchen to the hissing sound of water filling the dishwasher, and hopped up the stairs.

Every step she took was like a glimpse at her past. School pictures framed and carefully hung on the wall showed the six McKaslin girls, all blond and blue-eyed, alike as peas in a pod, smiling nearly identical smiles.

As she climbed toward the second story, the pictures grew older, marching through the years. To high school portraits in the hallway and Karen's and Kirby's wedding pictures. Everyone looked so happy and joyful, all the sisters crowded together in colorful bridesmaid dresses in both sets of wedding photos, but one sister was missing. Allison.

Nothing would ever be the same, she knew, as she stood before the final picture in the photo saga of the McKaslin family. Karen's newborn daughter, Allie was named in honor of the sister who had died so young.

What other pictures would follow, Michelle wondered? There would be more babies, more weddings. She had no doubt her two currently unmarried sisters would find love.

Would there be love for her? Or would she always be like this, running behind, left in the dust. She'd watched as her sisters were old enough to do what she couldn't: ride horses, ride bikes, go to school, become cheerleaders, go to the prom, go steady, marry a great guy.

She'd always felt as if she'd never caught up as her sisters grew up and left home. And in the grief of losing Allison, she'd felt like she'd lost her family, as well. The house that was once full now echoed around her as she made her way down the hall.

She supposed that's why she wanted to fall in love. To try and finally have what had been so wonderful and then slipped away. The warm tight cohesive love of a family and the happiness that came from it.

"Patience," Gramma was always telling her. "The good Lord gives us what we need at just the right time."

Well, how long would she have to wait? Her steps echoed through the lonely house that once had been filled with laughter and love.

She knew better than to hope that a stranger, a man passing through town on his way to a more exciting life, would be the one who could save her from this aloneness.

She was old enough to have stopped believing in fairy tales. But she wanted a happily-ever-after of her very own. She wanted a white knight on a fast horse with a heart strong and true.

That it was impossible. There weren't men like that in the world. Well, maybe the world, but absolutely certainly not in tiny, humble Manhattan, Montana.

She could see Brody's window from her bedroom. Just the corner of it, where a small light shone through the dark and the winds and rain. Her heart caught and remained a stark ache in the middle of her chest.

Brody would be moving on come morning. She knew it. That's why she was sad as she brushed her teeth, washed her face and changed into her pj's. The sadness deepened as she said her prayers and turned out the light.

It wasn't about Brody. That wasn't it. It was the promise of what he could be. Of what she wanted a man to be. Protective and disciplined and honest and strong. The kind of man who would never lie, never fail, never betray her and love her forever.

Were there men out there like that?

Only in fairy tales.

She drew her comforter up over her head and closed her eyes.

"I'm in." Brody kept the lights off as he sat on the little balcony deck, tucked beneath the awning just off the small apartment bedroom. "I took a spill on the bike, but—"

"Are you okay?" His partner sounded concerned.

"When haven't I been? I've crashed and burned before." He'd learned how to avoid serious injury during his training. He related the sequences of occurrences that had him bunked up in the McKaslins' spare apartment. "Banged up, but I'll survive. I don't have my pack with me, or I could start surveillance tonight."

"You're on the property? Man! Talk about Providence."

"No kidding." Hunter Takoda was a good partner, the best of the best, and they'd worked together for the past five years.

"Your footwork paid off. I'm going to head out tonight, once the lights are out and everyone's bedded down for the night—"

He heard the crunch of tires on gravel, and high

beams upon the driveway cast spears of light around to the back of the garage, where he was.

Because of years of being partnered together, Brody didn't need to tell Hunter that he had to check something out. Hunter waited patiently on the other end of the secure call while Brody limped through the dark apartment as fast as he could go, stubbed the toe of his injured foot on the leg of the coffee table, bit back the gasp of pain and crouched in front of the windows.

He heard the garage doors crank open as a big gray car—the one registered to Mrs. Alice Mc-Kaslin—drove into the garage beneath him and out of sight. He heard the engine die, and the garage doors eased downward.

A tidy, well-kept woman in her fifties, wearing a dress and heels, tapped down the walk to the front porch, opened the door and disappeared inside. Lights flashed on in the kitchen windows, but the blinds were drawn.

"I'm going out tonight. I'll rough out the property. There's got to be a few more service roads around here than I could find on the map. McKaslin's moving the money somehow."

"Think it's a family operation, like the last case we busted over in Idaho?"

Brody thought of Michelle's easy goodness. It was hard to see her engaging in criminal activity. "I may just have to spend some time ferreting that out for sure." Wasn't that too bad?

"Oh, I know. All those pretty blond women."

Hunter laughed. "Yeah, I did the original surveil-lance. I know what you're thinking. When was the last time we got to work with really pretty women?"

"Really pretty and really decent women don't have a tendency to garner the FBI's interest." Brody hoped Hunter wouldn't figure out the truth—that he had a personal interest in Michelle.

Interest. That's as far as it could go. He could secretly like her, what did that hurt? As long as he kept his objectivity. He was a professional. He was the best in the agency at what he did.

He'd finish this job the right way.

Chapter Four

As Michelle saw it, there were only two problems with having a horse. One was that she had to get up every morning at five to feed and water Keno and change his bedding. And the second problem was that the stable was in the *opposite* direction of the garage.

"Stop that, Keno." She flicked her ponytail out of his mouth and gave him a sharp glare; the one that said, cross me and you'll regret it.

Except that everyone, even her horse, already knew the real her. Ever playful, Keno shook his big head from side to side. The instant she bent back to work, he tugged on her ponytail again.

"All right, all right. I *know*." Michelle rescued her hair and leaned the pitchfork against the side wall of the stall. "I've got things to do, I don't have time to let you order me around this morning."

Keno, her best friend ever, knew when he had the

advantage and moved in to cinch the deal. He leaned
the length of his nose against her sternum and stomach, as if to say he loved her. And what was a girl
going to do about that?

Michelle melted like hot gooey chocolate left in
the sun and gave her horse a hug back. "Okay, okay,
you win."

The big dark bay shook his black mane and nickered in excitement. This is what she got for ignoring
him yesterday. "It wasn't as if you were neglected,
you big baby. You had the other horses to keep you
company."

The poor, neglected gelding stood still while she
snapped the blue lead rope onto his matching nylon
halter and led him through the wide stall door into
the pasture.

What a great morning for a ride. The morning was
fresh and the breeze sweet and warm as the new sun
welcoming her. As boring as it was living in small-
ville, *this* was worth it. Freedom sparkled all around
her, and she laughed at the nuzzle of Keno's whis-
per-soft lips against her face.

She buried her left hand in his sturdy mane and
braced the other on his back. She hopped on, pulled
herself astride. Keno shifted with her weight, holding back all his power and energy until she sent him
into an easy lope that made his mane dance and the
meadow speed by.

She hadn't ridden him yesterday, and he stretched
his legs now as she leaned forward, gripped him

hard with her thighs, and urged him into a faster run. But to where?

She could nose him into the rays of the rising sun and take him on the river trail, as she often did, or she could circle him around along the fence line. Yep, that's what she'd do. Because from the rise near the house, she'd get a good look at the garage. She'd be able to see if Brody was up yet.

And if he was, she'd invite him in to meet her parents. And since she had several clients this morning, she'd take him with her on her way to town and connect him up with his bike. That way she'd at least be able to say goodbye to him before he rode off forever.

Speaking of goodbyes, there was her dad's truck. The old tan-and-white pickup lumbered down the driveway and kicked up a soft plume of dust into the clean morning air.

Dad was going to town? He was usually in the fields this time of morning, checking the crops and irrigation equipment. There were always a thousand things to keep him busy.

But to head to town? Nothing was open, not even the coffee shop.

Brody. The realization pierced through her chest, leaving a physical pain. Surely Mom and Dad found the note she'd left, detailing the events that led to the stranger staying the night in the garage apartment, and Dad was taking charge, like always. He was taking Brody into town.

What? Without getting to say goodbye to him? As if!

Michelle signaled Keno to stop. At the crest of the knoll closest to the house, she could see the garage and the windows above it. The blinds were open, so that meant that Brody was obviously up. Thanks to the low angle of the sun, she could see right into the apartment. No one was there.

Sadness ripped through her, sharp as a razor blade. And how could that be? She'd only know Brody for what, like thirteen hours, and most of those she'd been asleep. So why did she feel so sad? As if she'd lost something of immense value? It made no sense.

He was gone. She laid the heel of her palm over her heart, wishing the sadness would stop. *Watch over him, Father. Keep him safe on his journey. Help him find whatever he's searching for.*

Michelle swore she could hear the faintest answer, but the wind gusted and the seed-heavy grass rattled before she could grasp the words.

It was as if the sun had gone down on her, and how much sense did that make? But that's what it felt like as she walked Keno back, cooling him off before she brushed him down in the gentle warmth of the rising sun.

Maybe it was the promise of a man like Brody. The hope of what she wanted in her life. A big strong man who was a little tough, looked a little dangerous, who was unique. A rugged individual. A good man of faith with a gentle heart.

There had to be men like that *somewhere* in the world. All she wanted was the right man. The best man. Someone she could love with all her heart.

Yeah, like they just fell out of the sky like rain.

She checked the water in the trough, poured grain, forked fresh alfalfa into the feeder and gave Keno one last hug before she locked the stall gate after her. She hadn't felt this lonely in a long time, so why now?

Her steps echoed in the stable, melancholy sounding. She remembered when the stalls were full, and her sisters were always around, coming and going, cleaning stalls or grooming their horses. Now there was only the brush of dawn at the open doors as she stepped out into the morning alone.

Meeting Brody had done this. It made her wish— for one impossible second—that her life could change. That she could find love and a family of her own. That she would be able to be loved and to love, to give her soul mate all the love she'd been saving up in her heart just for him.

Whoever he was.

Well, not Brody. That was for sure.

At least it was Friday. She'd better remember to give her sisters a call—well everyone but Kristin because she lived in Seattle—and set up a game tonight. It was her turn to host. What was she gonna do for food?

They could barbecue, but then she was a disaster when it came to Dad's propane grill. She'd set the cobs of corn on fire last time. She wasn't the best cook, so she didn't want to torture her sisters with some lame casserole. Wait, maybe she'd pick up a take-and-bake pizza from town. Perfect.

Feeling a little better, she kicked off her boots at the back steps and skidded to a stop in the threshold.

There, seated at the round oak table in the kitchen's sunny eating nook was a dark-haired man. She recognized the tousled shanks of hair and the long powerful curve of his shoulder and back.

Brody. He was here? He hadn't left?

Her knees felt unsteady, so she leaned against the door frame realizing too late that she'd swept her sleep-rumpled hair into a ponytail, and she hadn't showered. Without makeup, and wearing a pair of old cut-offs, she had to look totally gross. She had to smell like her horse.

She was afraid Brody was going to leap out of his chair in horror and run on his injured ankle for the hills.

She couldn't blame him if he did.

"Here, Michelle, honey." Her mom noticed her first as she turned from the stove. "You're just in time. Do you have a full morning at the Snip & Style?"

"Yeah." Somehow she managed to talk like a normal person—with consonants and vowels and words and everything. "I'm, uh, didn't know Brody was here."

It was the nicest surprise *ever*.

He twisted in the chair, hooking his arm around the ladder back, looking like a dream come true as he smiled. Slow. Steady. "Your mom offered me breakfast and I'm not about to turn down a home-cooked meal. Mrs. McKaslin, I can't remember when I've had such a privilege."

"Goodness, you're awfully well mannered for a biker." Michelle's mom tried to look stern, but pink blushed her face as she set two more plates on the table. She was pleased with the compliment. "Call me Alice. Michelle, I put your plate in the oven to keep warm. Mick's is in there, too."

"He's not with Dad?"

"He's not up yet. He's not answering his phone, anyway."

Michelle knew better than to say anything more. She grabbed a hot pad from the hook on the wall and found her plate in the oven. Uncle Mick was a sore point in the family. Her stomach tightened with worry over it as she headed to the table.

"Who's Mick?" Brody asked, absently, as if to make conversation in the suddenly tense silence.

"My uncle." Michelle dropped into the chair closest to him. "He's going through a divorce and lost his job, so Dad hired him on to help out this summer."

"Hmmph!" was the only comment Alice McKaslin made as she switched the burners and set the frying pan heavy with hot grease on a trivet to cool.

Brody quirked his left brow.

Michelle *knew* his question. She didn't even need to ask. How weird was that? "Uncle Mick is Dad's favorite brother. I was named after him. I was sup-

posed to be a boy, so they named me Michelle instead of Michael. Anyway, Uncle Mick's not the
most responsible of men. He's a rad uncle, but
he's—''

''—never grown up, and that's not attractive in a
forty-nine-year-old man.'' Her mother's stern look
said everything. ''Now, it's time for grace.''

Michelle clasped her hands and bowed her head
during the prayer. As she whispered an *amen,* she
looked at Brody and wondered. Was it chance that
he'd landed here? Or was he part of a bigger plan?

He looked noble with his high proud cheekbones
and the slant of his straight nose. He sat straight in
the chair, head bowed forward as he added a silent
prayer to the end of her mother's grace.

Okay, she *had* to like him even more for that—if
it was possible to like him any more than she already
did. He was so sincere and faithful as he muttered
an *amen* and reached for his fork. He looked a little
sheepish as he caught her watching him.

''I always say a prayer for my mom and dad.
They're in heaven.'' He shrugged as if a little embarrassed.

Could he be more perfect?

''Brody,'' Alice said as she poured a glass of
milk, ''where are you from? That's some accent
you've got.''

''Me? I thought I'd gotten rid of that. I've lived
in the West so long, it's practically gone.'' He shook
his head when Alice offered him the creamer. He
lifted the steaming cup of coffee by his plate and

sipped. Savored. Swallowed. "Sure is good, ma'am. I'm from West Virginia."

"Goodness. That sure is a long ways from here. Did you live there long?"

"Born and raised." Brody dug into the delicious-looking hash browns—so buttery and golden crisp and made from real shredded potatoes. He took it as another sign he was on the right path. "I'm a country boy at heart, even though I moved to the city when I was twelve."

"Was that in West Virginia, too?"

"Yes, ma'am." He felt the steel around his heart harden. There were a lot of things he didn't like to think too much about. Spending his teen years in a boys' home for lack of foster care was one of them. He cleared his throat, tried to keep his mind focused. To not let the sadness of his past effect the quality of his present life.

"Mom, you're being nosy again." Michelle's eyes sparkled with those little glints of blue sapphire that could captivate the most professional, dedicated agent. "You don't have to give us your life history. Where are you headed next when you get your bike?"

"I don't rightly know." That was the truth. He was ready to go on about how he'd be heading up to Glacier, that was the background story he'd hatched up, but the truth sidetracked him.

He had vague ideas about what he wanted to do when he left, but he didn't have a set plan. It bothered him. The past ten years at the Bureau had been demanding work—long hard hours, constant travel, tough assignments and dangerous missions.

It wore on a man. Chiseled at his soul.

He believed in the power of prayer. He figured he'd leave it in God's hands. That the good Lord would point him in the right direction.

"Surely you have family back in West Virginia. You're eventually headed back there?" Alice McKaslin prompted.

"I don't have any family."

"What? No family?" Tenderhearted Michelle sat wide-eyed, watching him carefully.

His heart stopped beating. Why was he reacting to her this way? Just because she looked like everything right in the world, with her hair tied back in that bouncy ponytail and her honest face more beautiful without a hint of makeup, it didn't mean that he should notice her.

He was on a mission. He needed to stay focused.

Right. His mission. Where was he? What did he need to do? Oh, that's right. You'd think he was a green agent getting his feet wet on his first assignment with the way he was acting. Good thing the surveillance equipment wasn't installed yet or Hunter would be getting a good laugh about now.

Focus, Agent Brody. Focus. He took a big bite of delicious scrambled eggs, getting a good rein on his thoughts while he chewed.

Alice McKaslin focused on her daughter. "You be sure and tell Nora that I say hello. I've missed her at the Ladies' Aid. I hardly see her now that she's busy with her new grandbabies.''

''Here it comes again.'' Michelle rolled her eyes, as if she knew exactly where her mother was going with this. ''I know, only two of your daughters are married, with only one baby between them.''

''It's not right, that's what! I raised you girls better than that. I want grandchildren.'' Alice Mc-Kaslin's eyes were twinkling as she held back a dignified smile. ''Nora has three grandchildren of her own, and three step-grandchildren.''

''It's a hint. Like I'm supposed to be desperate enough to marry Bart, the farmer guy next door, who keeps trying to ask me out. Just so she can have a few more grandchildren to cuddle. As if!''

Alice gave him the eye. ''And tell me why it is you haven't married? You'd think a man your age would want to settle down and have a family.''

''I haven't met the right woman yet.'' Why did his gaze flick to Michelle?

''So, you're looking?'' Alice gave him a careful nod, as if he maybe—just maybe—might pass muster with her.

''Looking, but it's tricky to find the right match. Someone who is right for you in every way.'' And wasn't that a little too personal? It took all his willpower not to look at Michelle, even though he felt the power of her presence as tangible as the floor at his feet. As the bandage on his forehead.

Time for a change of subject. ''So, Michelle. I bet you're a good stylist.''

"I do my best, but as I mentioned yesterday it takes a long time to get a good clientele built up. Especially in a town where you grew up in and everybody remembers every dumb thing you ever did."

"You don't look as if you could do one dumb thing."

Alice coughed delicately into her hand. "You don't know our Michelle."

Michelle rolled her eyes in mock agony as she scooped her serving of eggs on one slice of toast. "You turn your sister's hair green once and nobody forgets it. Three years later, and people are still saying, 'Now don't you go turning my hair green like you did your sister's.'"

Brody struggled not to laugh. That wasn't in his Intel report.

"And these are people of faith! You'd think they'd know how to forgive. I'm never going to live it down. When I'm an old maid of sixty-nine trying to build up to full-time, people are *still* going to be talking about it."

"Haven't I always said a girl's reputation is beyond price?" Her mom actually smiled.

Michelle's fork tumbled from her fingers. Her mother had had a difficult time with depression since Allison's death. And to see her looking almost happy made Michelle want to jump up and give thanks.

She recovered her fork instead, choosing to thank the Lord quietly, and she rolled her eyes again when she saw Brody watching her with a quirked brow and a crooked grin. "All right, I am a little klutzy. I've been rumored to be a walking disaster, but those tales are largely exaggerated."

"I'm glad to hear it. When I was driving up this way, folks would warn me about this blond-haired woman who lived north of Manhattan who was an F-5 tornado disaster. To keep clear of her. I can see I wasn't spared, even when I was trying to pass you on the highway."

"Ha ha. I had nothing to do with your accident."

"Tell that to my lawyer." He winked.

"I'll settle out of court, as long as you agree to let me keep my shoe collection."

"That's her entire net worth," her mom quipped.

"That's not true. Well, almost." Michelle thought of her impulse purchases upstairs, still in their original boxes. What a shame she hadn't time to add them to her closet. She felt a pinch of remorse, but she'd worry about her budget later.

"Speaking of which, I've got to shower and change if I don't wanna be late!" Michelle stuffed two strips of bacon on her eggs on toast and folded it over into a sandwich.

Well, there was no more procrastinating, no way to draw out the morning. There was a handsome stranger at her kitchen table and she had to go. It was her Christian duty, of course, to help him as much as she could, right? "Do you want to ride to town with me?"

"I'm not so sure. I was hoping that before your family booted me out on my ear, I'd be able to repay their hospitality.'' Brody wiped his plate clean with the last of his toast. ''Is there anything I can do around here, Mrs. McKaslin? Something your husband is too busy running the farm to do for you?''

''Oh, my dear man. You have no idea!'' Her mom lit up like a thousand-watt bulb. ''But you're injured. You couldn't possibly do much.''

''My ankle's wrapped. I'm a quick healer.''

Brody's wink made Michelle shiver. All the way to her toes. Wasn't it just too bad he might be hanging around for a little while longer? ''Put him to work and make him suffer, Mom. I have a feeling he deserves it.''

''Me? What did I do?'' But he was chuckling, a warm rich wonderful sound that could make a girl dream.

''Later.'' She escaped while she could, dashing up the stairs and trying not to think of the...possibilities.

Chapter Five

Hunter didn't bother to say hello, he picked up the phone in the middle of the first ring. "You're late checking in, buddy."

"Sorry about that. Unavoidable." Brody, with the phone tucked in one hand, carried the full can of paint out of the corner of the garage and into the shade outside. "Mrs. McKaslin has me busy. I've changed lightbulbs, repaired a window blind, fixed the ice maker on the refrigerator and now I'm painting their garage."

"All of that, and it's not five o'clock yet?"

"Their day starts at 4:30 a.m."

"Wicked." Hunter laughed. "Still hangin' in there? How's your ankle?"

"Killing me, but that's okay. I'll ice it tonight. It's endeared me to Mrs. McKaslin. She baked me a chocolate cake."

"Couldn't do better. Look, I've got the drop taken

care of. The surveillance equipment is in a storage place just east of town. I'll leave a starter bag on your balcony some time after dark.''

"Good. It sounds like most of the family is going to be gone. It's Friday night. The missus has a church function, which her husband will be showing up to later. Michelle probably has a date. The way Alice talked, she worried that I'd be on my own.''

"We shouldn't have any problem. If you can handle it on your end, I'll set up a tail on Mick. I'm pulling some agents from the Bozeman office to help me out.''

"All two of them?'' It was a small office, and in a small population base they had to worry about being recognized. A stranger's face stuck out in a small town. So did a strange vehicle tailing a suspect on a road with no traffic for miles. "I called the mechanic in town. He's got a part coming overnight, and I should have my wheels back soon.''

"That's one problem solved. Be careful tonight, Brody.'' Hunter turned serious. "Remember the Misu Flats case? Started out like this, nice as pie. Sweet grandmother type who surprised us by sending two hired hit men to kill us in our sleep.''

"I get the hint. You be careful, too, buddy.'' He heard the sound of a rattling engine and he signed off. Tucked the phone in the back pocket of his cutoffs and went to work removing the empty can and replacing it with the full one.

Michelle, he figured, without turning around, and

wasn't surprised when her vehicle pulled into the carport on the other side of the garage.

"Careful!" He called out when he heard the hinges of the truck's door squeak open. "Wet paint."

"Mom has been putting you to work. Are you sure you're up to this?" Michelle's sandals clacked on the concrete. The sound of plastic bags rustling had him looking up.

And admiring the prettiest girl he'd ever seen. He'd seen beauty—who hadn't?—but deep down loveliness, the kind that came from within, was something a man didn't come across every day.

Her hair was tied back in a single decorative braid, and her short, wispy bangs framed her face. She wore little makeup, just on her lashes so thick and long, and a hint of color on her lips. Fresh-faced and lovely, she smiled her genuine smile.

The kind without guile. Without guilt. Without falsehood. The kind he didn't see too often in his line of work.

He snagged the empty paint can and headed her way. "What? You're concerned about me now, are ya? Wasn't it you who said that I deserved to be put to work and made to suffer?"

"Sure, what man doesn't?" Trouble twinkled in her eyes.

He could be trouble, too. "I suppose it's a woman's duty in life to make a man suffer."

"Sure, it is. What else are men for?"

"Changing lightbulbs. Painting garages. Making credit card payments."

"Exactly. Oh, you missed a spot."

"Thanks. I wouldn't have noticed that spot being half of the entire wall without you."

"Happy I could help." She slid her sunglasses on and clicked away, her shopping bags rustling.

"Got any food in there for me?" he called after her.

She didn't even turn around. "Nope. We planned on starving you."

Why was he laughing? Why was he feeling like he was not on assignment?

Get back to work, Brody, and stop flirting with the pretty lady. That was easier said than done, he thought, as he climbed the ladder. But he had painting to do, and a counterfeit money ring to break.

Was that the phone? Michelle tugged off the towel wrapped around her head. Her hair was still wet from a quick shower, and the terry cloth made it hard to hear.

The loud *brring* from downstairs confirmed it. In bare feet and with her hair all tangly and without a speck of makeup, she tore down the hall and down the stairs in time for the ringing to stop.

That's why the good Lord had invented caller ID. She checked the number on the little white box in the kitchen. She dialed and waited, figuring that Karen, her older sister, had called to ask what to bring tonight. Karen was like that, conscientious and wonderful, and Michelle missed having her around all the time. She didn't see Karen as much now that she'd had the baby and was only working part-time at the coffee shop, which she owned.

Karen answered on the first ring. "There you are! I was just about to try the coffee shop."

"Nope, I closed up. No problems." Michelle planted her elbows on the kitchen island and leaned forward, trying to get the best view out the window. If she looked just right, maybe she could see Brody. "Are you ready to get the socks beat off you tonight?"

"I wish, but that's why I'm calling."

"What?"

"I just got back from the clinic with the baby. Allie's got an ear infection and we can't come tonight. I'm sorry."

"Is she all right?" Michelle tried to set aside her disappointment. Her baby niece was ill, and that was what truly mattered.

"I've got some medicine in her, and Zach's rocking her. She's almost asleep." Affection and concern warred in Karen's voice. "The doctor assured me she'll be fine. I just worry."

"Me, too." Michelle thought of her precious little niece, so tiny and vulnerable. It was really something how families were made, children grew up and the cycle continued; sure, it was obvious, but the reassurance of it was like a piece of beauty in her life.

"Do you need me to do anything? I could run to

the store, if you need me to. Come over if you need a volunteer to rock her.''

"Thanks, sweetie. I'll let you know if we need you. Have a good time tonight and know I'm missing you all.''

"Not half as much as we'll miss you. Give Allie a kiss for me.''

The beep of the phone's off button echoed in the too-quiet kitchen. It was a big room. It was a big house. She felt so alone in it.

If she listened hard enough she could hear the echoes of memories, of good times. The morning sun streaking through the window as six girls dashed around the kitchen. Mom at the stove shouting orders. Dad trying to read his paper in peace.

There were arguments and chaos and laughter and inevitably a spilled glass of milk or juice. The squeals when Mom shouted out the time. "The bus'll be here any minute. You girls are going to be late if you don't hurry up!''

And they'd all squeal again, racing to find shoes, hair ribbons, library books or whatever else in the last flurry before they all shoved out the back door.

And now the house was so quiet. Sadness ached like a sore tooth inside her as she headed back upstairs, taking the phone with her. For everything there is a season, the Bible said, but the changing of those seasons brought with it a loss. Was what lay before her as good and as happy as the times behind?

As if in answer, the back door thudded closed,

and the sound drummed through the house. Was it Kirby? Or Kendra? Maybe it was Brody. She couldn't let him see her like this. Not again. She had to at least get her hair combed!

Yep, it was Brody, she figured, when no sister paraded through the house in search of her. In her room, Michelle ran a brush through her tangled locks, took some curly gel stuff and scrunched it into her hair and went in search of her favorite lipstick. Of course, it was downstairs. With her purse. She'd have to make do with Plum Sunrise. She grabbed the tube and applied it, hands trembling.

Okay, she had to admit she'd been hatching a plan all day. It had undergone many revisions, but she'd settled on one. To invite Brody to join them tonight, of course. She'd gotten an extra pizza, with the works on it, because he didn't look like a plain-cheese-pizza kind of guy.

Brody rinsed out the sprayer hose, put away the ladder and groaned on his way toward the family's two-story ranch house with the wide front porch and Victorian charm. Although Alice McKaslin had run off to her church meeting, she'd promised there were leftovers in the refrigerator he could help himself to. To make himself at home, use their large-screen television with the satellite dish. She'd said he'd certainly earned it with all his work today.

Work? Well, he was pleasantly tired as he rapped his knuckles on the back screen door. No answer,

but he went in anyway. Michelle was probably upstairs. He'd grab some ice and put up his feet and
rest his ankle for a bit. See what happened from
there.

He heard the phone ring, shrilling in the empty,
spacious kitchen. The handset was gone, so he sidled
close to where the base sat tucked at the end of the
kitchen's breakfast bar. He peeked at the caller ID
box. Kirby and Sam Gardner. He recognized that
name. Another one of Michelle's older sisters, married and living in town.

The ringing stopped. He could hear the distant rise
and fall of Michelle's cheerful voice from her room
upstairs. He knew the name because he'd gotten a
good look at the house while doing handiwork for
Alice McKaslin today. Curious, he hit the caller ID's
back button and read the list of names. There were
names he recognized; one was the name and number
on his suspect list. Lars Collins.

The question was, who had made that call to Lars?
He'd requested phone records, and he was still waiting on the warrant. He knew there were possibly
other calls. Mick had so far made no long-distance
calls from his current phone. Were more of the
McKaslins involved? Or was Mick using this phone,
wise enough to use different phones.

Brody didn't need to write down the list and numbers. He memorized them before taking a step toward the refrigerator. He spied Michelle's purse
tossed on the counter. Keys, a few greenbacks, her

wallet and a tube of lipstick had spilled out of the open zipper, as if she'd tossed it there in a hurry to unload the grocery bags he remembered that she'd been carrying.

When it came to Michelle, he remembered a lot. The way she walked—quick and fluid, like liquid gold. And how quick she was to smile. He was impressed by how nice she was, and she didn't even seem to be aware of it. That was a rare woman, in his experience.

He closed off bad memories of terror and cruelty he'd seen over the years, and the weight of it hurt inside him. Like a wound too often reinjured to heal. It was heartening to see goodness, for a change. He knew that during the course of his investigation he would find nothing to incriminate Michelle. She was too good. And it made something in his closed-off heart brighten. As if touched by sunshine for the first time.

Maybe he'd spend some time here. Figure out if Michelle had any plans for the evening. She'd brought food home; she didn't have a date? He hoped not. The center of his chest warmed with the intensity of a grow light, and it was an odd thing.

He reached into the top cupboard for a glass. Sure, he used to date, but he was never in one place long enough to keep a relationship going. It had always made him sad, but he'd known he wouldn't be doing investigative work forever. It was a noble cause he served, and he figured there would be time later for love and commitment and family. If he was ever lucky enough.

Not that he was thinking in that direction, but—

He looked down. A serial number caught his attention. The folded twenty-dollar bill had only part of the sequence visible, poking out of Michelle's wallet the way it was.

His jaw dropped. The blood in his veins turned to ice. The warmth in his chest faded into darkness. He inched the twenty-dollar bill out enough so that he could verify the number. Grabbed his cell phone, glanced over his shoulder to make sure he was alone and that the lilting mumble of Michelle's voice was still coming from her bedroom overhead, before taking a picture with the camera on his phone.

Documented. He felt sick in his stomach, sick in his soul. He carefully checked the rest of her cash stuffed haphazardly in the expensive leather wallet. There was one other twenty, hidden between a five and three crumpled ones, but it was legit.

Just because she had a counterfeit bill didn't mean she was guilty. It could have been passed to her in a number of ways. Those bills were in circulation around town and around Bozeman. Both places where she'd been recently.

Be real, Brody. You just don't want to believe Michelle could be a criminal. Innocent-seeming Michelle, who made even his battle-scarred heart begin to feel.

Evidence. That's what he was here to discover. And he'd just found a big piece of it.

* * *

Michelle just knew it was bad news. "No, don't even tell me. You're going to cancel tonight. Again."

"I'm sorry. You know Karen has the same problem."

"I know." Michelle rolled her eyes. She wasn't mad or anything, but she couldn't be more disappointed. "It's the husband factor. I know. You have to spend some time with him. It's ridiculous, and I *can't* understand why—"

The way she said it, with just enough teasing to hide her true feelings, made Kirby laugh.

"I know I cancelled last week for that very reason, but I have a much better excuse this time." Kirby turned serious. "I received a medi-vac call about a half second ago. I'm on my way to the airstrip. Sam's holding the chopper for me."

Someone was seriously ill or hurt. How could Michelle begrudge them her sister? "You two fly safe. Call me tomorrow when you get up, okay?"

"I promise. Gotta go!"

At least Kendra was still coming. Michelle realized it would just be the two of them—the old maids of the family. And she'd bought two whole pizzas. That was wrong. Pizza couldn't go to waste. Wasn't it good that she intended to do the right thing and invite Brody to join them?

That made her smile as she blow-dried her hair, and chose a new pair of sandals to go with her favorite carpenter shorts and her new eyelet, V-necked top. She grabbed the phone and clipped on her gold bracelet her dad had given her when she graduated from high school as she headed down the hall.

Should she pick a movie or music for background noise? A movie, definitely, she thought as she descended the stairs. She'd pick a favorite romantic comedy, one they'd seen a few times before so they could listen without having to watch.

She walked into the living room. The TV was on. Did she do that? She couldn't remember turning it on, but then she forgot a lot of stuff.

The chair moved and she squealed. For one split second fear paralyzed her and then she recognized the man's chiseled form sitting half hidden in her dad's recliner. "Brody! You scared me to death. I didn't know you were here."

"I didn't know I was so scary just sitting in the recliner."

He sat calm and self-possessed as he took a drink from one of her mom's flowery brown-and-yellow glasses. Ice cubes tinkled as he drank long. The strong column of his throat worked as he swallowed and set the glass aside. All he had to do was smile, and her pulse was still racing. She couldn't slow it down. How crazy was that? As if her heart rate was ever going to be normal around him!

But she could try to *seem* normal. She spotted a bag of frozen green peas draped over his propped-up ankle. "How's your ankle feeling?"

"It's protesting, but I'm tough."

"And the bag of green peas is, what, a fashion statement?"

He shrugged one wide shoulder but he looked away and not directly at her. "I didn't want to snoop in the drawers looking for a zipper-seal plastic bag, so I borrowed this from the freezer. What are you up to?"

"No good, as usual."

"Is that right? A nice girl like you?"

"Yep. I'm planning a night of wild partying and reckless wrongdoing. Are you interested?"

She *had* to be kidding, Brody figured. With the way she knelt in front of the entertainment cabinet and studied the very wholesome movies there. "Sure. Count me in. I'm a wild kind of guy."

"Even with that ankle slowing you down, huh?" Michelle leaned forward to study the titles, golden hair tumbling forward, shiny and beautiful. After some debate, she selected a movie. "How do you feel about pizza?"

"I've been known to eat a slice or two. Or three. Or twelve."

"Pepperoni?"

"What other kind is there?"

"Ah, a man after my own heart." Michelle felt her face flame. Could she have said anything more embarrassing? She tried hard to act casual. "How about sausage?"

"Onions, green peppers, you name it. I'll be glad to eat it and give thanks."

"Good. I understand if you're not interested, but if you're a courageous man who isn't afraid of danger and intrigue, then you can join me and my sisters for our weekly gathering. Dinner and, since it's my turn to pick the board game, a rousting round of Scrabble.''

Brody's ankle slipped off the pillow and he sat up with a bang. The bag of peas dropped to the floor. ''I'm a Scrabble buff.''

''You're kidding.''

''No.'' Who would have guessed this? He forgot about his sore ankle, the revolver tucked in the back of his Levis and that Michelle was in possession of counterfeit cash he was here to investigate. Excitement seized hold of him. ''I've played since I was a kid. My brother and I, we were just a year apart—''

He stopped as a dull ache tore through him. How could he have forgotten? How could he be getting carried away like this? He hadn't thought of Brian in years, and on purpose. He'd been killed in the car accident that had taken their parents.

It was easier to focus on the mission, and keep the pain in his heart locked behind closed steel doors. He took a steadying breath and rescued the sack of vegetables from the carpet.

Think about the mission. Remember where you are and what you are doing. He studied the bag of peas in his hands, still cold. *I need to get close to Michelle because she could be a criminal. Got that?* This was his opportunity and he intended to make the best of it.

''I got a knack for Scrabble, and I've played all my life. A buddy of mine—'' really his partner

"—and I play a couple times a week when we can. I've gotten pretty good over the years. It's only fair to warn you. I'm a dangerous man."

"Oh, like I'm scared." She turned a pretty shade of pink as she straightened, a movie case in hand. "I hope with that huge ego of yours that you'll survive losing to me."

"I won't lose."

"Okay, believe what you want. Cling to desperate hope if it makes you feel better." Michelle tried to pretend like she wasn't totally losing it around him, even though her hands were shaking as she set the movies on the top of the big screen TV her dad had bought to watch football.

She could see Brody perfectly. "Do you mind if I turn this on?"

"Go ahead." He stepped closer and watched her.

She could see him out of the corner of her eye, the way he stood as immovable and as impressive as a marbled statue. A wing of dark hair tumbled rebelliously over his forehead, making him look like a dangerous man gone good—barely.

Was he something or what? He made the room feel different, and she felt as skittish as her father's favorite mare during a thunderstorm. Brody's just a guy like any guy, she argued as she searched for the DVD remote.

Wrong. Brody was different from any man she'd ever met. He was the ideal dream of a man she saw when she closed her eyes in prayer asking for the perfect man to love for the rest of her life. Her palms were damp and she felt tingly in the middle of her spine. Looking at him made her hear Pachebel's Canon in D and envision the bouquet of roses and lilies she intended to carry the day she walked down the aisle. What good was that?

He was going to leave tomorrow on his sleek, expensive motorcycle and speed right out of her life forever.

There was the remote! She unburied it from beneath the TV schedule and clicked on the player.

"Your family has a few pictures on the wall."

"A few?" Michelle knelt in front of the entertainment center and inserted the disc. "More like thousands."

"There aren't that many."

"Okay, hundreds."

"You were pretty cute in that one without your front top teeth. And pigtails."

"Great. Thanks for mentioning that."

Brody still couldn't believe it. He'd seen the counterfeit bill with his own eyes, and it was hard to believe Michelle would be involved in something like that. It wasn't just because she was beautiful, it was something more. Something deeper.

He was wrong to want her to be innocent when he needed to keep his cool. Stay objective. Stick to his mission objectives. It was his duty to find evidence if she was involved and send her to prison.

He watched Michelle hit the play button, and in a few seconds the big black FBI warning flashed on the TV screen, and he took a step back.

Maybe beneath that girl-next-door freshness lurked the mind of a conscienceless criminal. It was his job to find out.

Then she straightened, and her big innocent eyes focused right on him.

"I'm sorry. I grabbed a romantic comedy out of habit. Kendra has been wanting to see this one again—like for the tenth time." She waved a DVD box with the picture of a smiling couple in the air. "I could check the dish listing and see if there's something more macho on. Like action adventure. But one without any blood and gore and violence. Ooh, and anything embarrassing. I guess they don't usually make those PG."

"Not usually."

She blushed, as if the prospect of the stage intimacy on screen embarrassed her beyond all belief. He turned away while she put the movie on Pause and switched the screen over to the local station. A friendly news anchor was announcing the future on wheat and soybeans.

The phone rang, and Michelle reached for the handset she'd left on the coffee table. "Hello?"

She cradled the receiver against her left ear, and she cocked one foot, listening with care. There was elegance to her and an understated class. There was no mistaking her wholesome beauty.

Everything within him beat with longing. When she breathed, he breathed. When her smile faded, so did his. She folded a golden lock of hair behind her ear. The glint of sunlight on the curve of her hoop earring was nothing compared to her beauty. He shouldn't be noticing her beauty.

Sadness touched her porcelain-fine features. Whom was she talking to? She was so expressive, how could she be hiding a life of crime?

"I understand, Kendra. Don't worry. I'm fine. Call me when everything's okay, will ya?" Michelle's chin dipped as she ended the call. She looked vulnerable, while trying not to show it. And failing.

His conscience was bothering him, and why was that? He'd never had this problem before. He'd done nothing wrong. He was doing his job. He didn't need to feel bad about suspecting a nice, sweet girl, who looked about as guilty as Marcia Brady.

"That was Kendra, my other sister." Michelle's smile was bright, but her eyes remained shadowed. Sad. And so was the false note in her voice. "She's bailing, too. One of her prized mares is having a hard time foaling, and Kendra has to stay. I'm praying mother and baby will be fine."

"What about the other sister?" He gestured to the framed group picture on top of the end table between the recliner and one of the couches. A family picture from last Christmas, he figured, since all five sisters were crowded together in front of a decorated tree. "She's not coming, either?"

"That's Kristin, and she's moved out of state. The only one of us with any sense." Her attempt at a joke failed, but at least it gave her time while she crossed the room and pulled the movie disc from the player.

As she placed it into its case, Michelle prayed for her sisters tonight, for her niece who was ill and her sister who was flying in turbulent weather and for Kendra's beloved mare.

All things change, she told herself, and so would this loneliness, too. One day there would be a husband of her own and a busy life to manage.

"You said that your sister's the only smart one," Brody asked. "Do you think that she was smart to leave? You don't like living here?"

"I thought about moving to L.A. or New York City, but after living here watching the grass grow all my life, I thought those cities might be a little dull for me."

"I've lived in those cities. They have their pluses and their minuses. But here—" He gestured to the wide picture window that offered a stunning view of the rugged Rockies with their jagged lavender peaks stabbing into the harsh gray of threatening clouds. "It's a piece of paradise."

Yes. In that moment, it felt as if her heart opened up. As if the secret wishes within her shimmered like stardust begging to be revealed.

How did she tell Brody? How would a man like him understand? He boldly followed his whims. Whenever he wanted to travel, he hopped on his powerful bike. He was a man of the world.

Sure, he hadn't said a single thing about it, but it showed. She could see he was a rugged loner. If he knew the truth about her, he'd probably just laugh at her. Like everyone else would. He might look out of her living room window and see heaven, but he wouldn't understand.

She had dreams. She had passions. She had goals she wanted to reach. And they mattered to her. She doubted a world-wise man would understand.

She stalked out of the room and away from Brody, leaving both her sadness and her dreams behind.

Chapter Six

Did he stay in the living room? No. He had to follow her into the kitchen when she wanted to be alone. His gait might be uneven due to his injured ankle as he padded over the carpeting and onto the linoleum, but there was no mistaking the confidence of his step and his sheer masculine power.

Why was it that when she *wanted* a handsome, intriguing dream of a man in her kitchen, there wasn't one to be found anywhere.

But the one time she *didn't* want one in her kitchen, there he was, stalking toward her like a predatory lion while she was wrestling with the stubborn wrapping on the pizza.

"Need some help?" His deep baritone rumbled over her.

She wouldn't look up. He was not her dream. He was just some guy. That's what she was going to tell herself over and over until she believed it. "I'm doing just fine, thank you very much."

"You don't look fine to me."

"That's because I'm hungry."

He splayed his wide, sun-bronzed hands on the breakfast bar, leaning closer.

Her awareness of him doubled. It was as if there were no barriers, not even flesh and bone, and her heart was out in the open and vulnerable.

Why did he make her feel this way?

"I know you don't *need* my help, but I'd like to lend a hand just the same," he offered.

The way Brody was leaning against the counter seemed to shrink the entire room. Make her senses zero in on only him.

A new emotion she'd never felt before sparked to life in her chest. Something painful and powerful and life changing. Just like that, she could feel places in her heart she'd never known. Vulnerable and still bearing the scars from her last relationship.

Please, Father, she prayed as she yanked open the drawer in search of the scissors. *Help me to be wiser. Help me not to confuse friendliness with affection.*

She wanted a great man to marry. She didn't want to make the same mistake she'd made with Rick. That in the wanting, she got carried away with the dreaming of what could be and didn't see the signs in front of her. The small clues that should have warned her Rick had his own motives.

But what motives could Brody have? He was here by chance, not by design.

"You could dig out the pizza stone." She freed the pizza from its shrink-wrapping. "It's in the bottom drawer beneath the built-in oven."

"Sure thing."

He sounded happy to please, digging through the bottom drawer as if it were a perfectly natural thing to do.

Her dad didn't do anything in the kitchen. Uncle Mick, her favorite uncle ever, sat at the table and good-naturedly expected to be waited on.

Brody retrieved the stone and laid it on the counter as she read the instructions to find the right temperature for the oven and turned it on. "I've been on the road a long time. I've forgotten what a real home feels like."

"I told you. It's pretty boring here."

"You don't seem bored."

How could he know? "It's not a life people think is all that interesting. But I ride my horse every day. I watch the sun rise every morning. I go to bed at night on this land my great-grandfather homesteaded. And I feel…"

She dumped the pizza on the stone and turned away. It was dorky and she wasn't going to say it.

As she grabbed the pizza stone, his big hand covered hers. Held on. The link she felt was like touching a live wire, a zapping vibration of emotion. Of understanding.

It was in his heart, and she *felt* it.

"Complete," he finished her sentence.

The exact word she would have used. How could this be happening?

"It's really something, what you've got here." He removed his hand from hers and stepped away.

Taking a part of him with her. How could that be? It didn't make any sense, but that's how it felt. The deepest part of her being throbbed with too many emotions to name—loneliness and longing and loss mingled with hope and love and wishes.

Brody had done this, opened a door to a room in her heart, one she'd never known existed. Now it was all she could feel.

He crossed to the big bay window behind the table, and he somehow still had a hold of her.

A torrent of feeling flowed through her, as cold as snowmelt in a spring creek. And it was as if she could feel his loneliness. Feel how he longed for dreams, too. It was as tangible as the oven handle in her hand.

She slipped the pizza into the oven, the draft of heat attempted to dry the tears on her cheeks, but she feared nothing could. She swiped at the wetness with the backs of her hands and hoped the slap of her sandals on the floor hid the sound of her sniff. What was happening to her? Did Brody feel this, too?

He jammed his hands into his back pockets, and he stood as straight as a soldier. "Which horse is yours?"

"The dark bay is my Keno. Look, he's lifting his head, watching the house. He knows tonight is Friday, and I'm not going to be taking him for a run until later, and it always makes him cranky.''

''He's keeping watch for you.''

''Yep. We're old friends.''

''I know how that is.'' Brody could hear the affection in her voice. Feel it like sunshine on his skin. ''A horse can be your best friend.''

''Keno and I have been through a lot over the years. It's a bond I can't explain. We grew up together. Keno is a part of nearly every good memory I have. We know each other so well.''

''It's a good way to grow up.''

''It sure is.'' She didn't add how she'd loved her childhood. How one day she wanted to give that kind of life to her own children. To blond-haired little girls riding their horses in the vast meadows. ''It's a good way to live now.''

Longing. Brody didn't know why he felt it so strongly within. His personal feelings had no place when he was on the government's clock. He wanted to tell himself he'd do better pushing the line of questioning to find out what he needed to about Michelle. To uncover her as a clandestine participant in her uncle Mick's money printing scheme.

But he knew beyond a doubt she was no criminal. His heart told him so.

''Ring.'' Proud of herself, Michelle slipped the tiles from her tray onto the crowded board. ''Ooh, and a triple score square.''

''Good, solid move.'' Across the dining room table, pizza crusts on their plates pushed aside and forgotten, Brody studied her with unflinching eyes. A predator's gaze.

Sure, he may have come up with a few good words, but he was probably just lucky. He didn't know whom he was up against. She'd been playing since her sisters let her sit on phone books so she could reach the table.

"Take your time. No hurry," she told him.

"A good player never hurries." He winked at her. "It's the secret to winning the game."

"Sometimes a stall tactic means you don't have a word to play."

"Are you doubting me?" He quirked a brow in a challenge.

A challenge? She wasn't afraid of him. "Show me what you've got, Mr. Scrabble Expert."

A killer grin tugged at the corner of his mouth. He dropped two tiles on the board to spell *gun*.

"That's the best you can do?" Boy, weren't some men all ego? She pulled new tiles out of the bag and arranged them on her tray. Piece of cake. She was going to win hands down.

"I'm not through yet," he said, fitting two more letters on either end. *"Gunship.* That means I'm ahead."

Michelle's jaw dropped. That was more than luck. Her admiration for him rose a notch higher. "You show some skill."

"I tried to warn you." He held up both hands as if he were innocent.

So, this was a serious game. Fine. She could rise to the challenge. She slid *vow* into place. "Top that, mister."

"No problem." He added *loner* to the board. "I need more tiles. Hand me the bag."

Their fingers brushed, but it was more than the callused warmth of him she felt.

She'd been in love before, and it hadn't felt like this. Being with Rick had made her feel happy. Being with Brody was overwhelming. Why was that? What was it about *this* man? She kept thinking about him, and she had to stop herself from dreaming about him.

"Having trouble?"

No. She pushed a *c* in front of *rush* on the board. *Crush.* That's what she had. It was like she felt in high school, before Rick ever noticed her. That innocent hoping, that rush of longing for the ideal.

"Michelle, I think that move of yours proves than I'm superior." He laid down the missing tiles to make the word *superior.* "And a bonus square, too."

"This is war. Wait. Give me a minute." She studied her letters. As if she'd let him win. "There. Take that."

"*Bride?* And a triple score." Brody quirked one brow. "Impressed, but I'm not intimidated."

He was already moving his pieces into place. *Wolf.*

She took more tiles and organized them on her tray. She built *romance.*

Why did she keep coming up with the same theme?

Because she was enamored by the rogue Scrabble master across the table from her.

As if he could hear her thoughts, he frowned. Not an unhappy frown, but it was a thoughtful one. His tiles spelled out *bachelor.*

She studied her letters. She added three more. *love.*

He spelled *freedom.*

Wed.

Single.

They each wrestled in the bag for the last of the tiles.

"I'm ahead by two points." Brody arranged and rearranged his letters. "Just thought you should know. You're going to lose this match, Miss Mc-Kaslin."

"Pride goes before a fall, Mr. Gabriel." She sounded confident, but her tiles were an unfortunate combination of the dregs in the bag: *ULASOMT*

"Can't do it, can you?" When his words could have been triumphant, they were low and rumbling and intimate.

She shivered down to her soul. There was only one combination. Her mind was blanking. Sure, she could use a word like *mat* or *lout,* but it wouldn't give her enough points. The question was, did she want to save her dignity or win the game?

How could she let him win? There was no way

Michelle Alice McKaslin lost a game of Scrabble to a man! *Think, Michelle. Think.*

"I just need a minute," she said.

"Take five. Take ten. You still aren't going to beat me."

Did he say that just to provoke her? It worked. "Now I have no choice. Here it is."

She pushed the letters onto the board, shifting them next to an *E*, until they spelled *soulmate.*

Could she be any more embarrassed? With the way Brody's eyes were gleaming and the way he cleared his throat, she wondered if he had a better word.

He reached across the table and pushed a stray hair out of her eyes and tucked it behind her ear.

A sweet and caring gesture. Everything within her stilled. Had he guessed? Did he know she had a crush on him?

Then he chucked her chin, just like her dad used to do when she was sad. A platonic gesture.

Oh. The open door inside her closed. She watched, swallowing hard to hide her disappointment, as Brody spelled his last word.

"For the win," he said.

She looked down to see he'd spelled *zero.*

As in her chances of having him fall in love with a girl like her.

She smiled with all the dignity she had left. Nothing had ever cost her so much.

Brody couldn't get the sick feeling out of his stomach as he headed up the flight of stairs to his temporary home above the garage. Tonight was going great.

Right up until he'd blown it.

He shouldn't have touched her. It sure seemed to upset her. After he'd won the game, she'd offered him a gentle congratulations, adding that she never lost and it had been an honor to play with a player who challenged her. All the while deftly packing away the game.

He'd helped her—at least, he thought he did. He couldn't remember. There was a moment in time where all he'd been aware of was the glide of her gold chain bracelet along her slim, sun-bronzed wrist. The swing of her hoop earrings against the delicate curve of her face.

The way she made him feel forever in a single moment.

"You gotta stop this, man," he muttered to himself as he put his hand over his weapon, ready to draw it. Training, and ten years of habit, had him checking the apartment before he relaxed. Mick McKaslin was so far a no-show. Not at his house. Not on the McKaslin land. Not at his usual places in town.

Had someone tipped him off? The usual spotters were in place—airports, train stations and rental car agencies. Maybe they'd do a sweep of license plates at hotels. Try to track him down that way, unless he'd gone to ground. Either way, his mission was clear. He had surveillance to do on Mick's place.

Brody pulled out his cell and fired off a text message to Hunter. "Be here at midnight."

He opened the blinds that had been closed tight against the afternoon sun. The sun had disappeared behind dark thunderheads blanketing the sky. A movement in one of the windows caught his attention.

Michelle. She was yanking at the cord of her blinds, which appeared to be stuck. She unraveled them, yanked on them, untwirled them some more and pulled again. The blind went unevenly down and she gave up, turning the vinyl slats closed against the coming twilight.

She'd taken the movie upstairs with her, and he figured she had a television in her room.

He felt oddly sad that she'd retreated from the living room instead of staying there with him.

And was that professional?

Not one bit. He'd better get his head on straight if he wanted this mission to be a safe one. Things could get out of hand quick.

There was a pickup lumbering up the driveway, kicking up dust in its wake. Pete McKaslin. Brody watched and waited while the man who'd greeted him with reserve early this morning stopped his truck and climbed out.

"Dad!" Michelle must have heard his truck because she darted out of the house. "Did you get supper while you were in town? I can put a pizza in the oven."

"That'd be great, honey." Pete gave his youngest

daughter a reserved nod. "Smells like we're gonna get lightning. Did you put up the horses?"

"I was just going to." Michelle traipsed back up the steps and hesitated on the wide old-fashioned porch. "Do you want me to put coffee on for you, too?"

"Later, honey." Pete opened the hood of the trunk. "I've got some trouble. Got to get it figured out. Now go do your chores, sweetie."

Pete seemed out of sorts, his brows deeply furrowed and his frown intimidating as he bent over his work.

Nothing like a perfect opportunity. Brody couldn't see an industrious farmer like Pete being involved in a counterfeiting ring, but he'd seen more unbelievable things. He'd keep an open mind.

"Want me to help troubleshoot?"

Pete looked up. "Hey, Brody. Glad to see you're still here. The garage looks good."

"I told Alice I'd do the trim first thing in the morning."

"Sure do appreciate it. This time of year I'm working from dawn until dusk. Get behind on what needs done around here."

"I appreciate the place to stay. Your son-in-law Zach said my bike will be ready about noon, so I'll be out of your hair."

"You ain't in the way, son. You're more of a helping hand than that brother of mine. Did he show up here tonight?"

"Nope. Is this the uncle Mick I've been hearing about?"

"That'd be him. Everybody loves Mick." Pete's frown returned and he stared at the engine. "Now this is a problem I can solve. I hope."

"Need this for work tomorrow?" Brody understood.

"I've got hay to cut. It can't wait. This storm'll blow over, you can feel it, but might not be so lucky tomorrow night. You know something about mechanics?"

"Enough to get by on." Brody gave thanks for the assignment where he'd worked undercover in a repair shop in Boring, Oregon. "What kind of problem are you having?"

"Overheating. Went to town this morning, got my son-in-law to open up his garage for me to check it out. Nothing. He changed my hoses, flushed out the radiator, replaced a fuse and such, but figured I might have to take it to the dealership. All those fancy computer chips they've got now days."

"Yep." Brody had to give high marks to the mechanic's work he saw. Neat and very competent. "An electrical problem?"

Pete wiped his face, as though the thought of it made him profoundly weary. A farmer's life was one of long hours and hard work, and it showed on this man who, by the look of it, had done it all his life. "Be right back."

Brody leaned against the truck while Pete disappeared into the depths of the roomy garage. The rising wind gusted across his face, hot and humid and bringing with it the fresh scent of mown grass. Of drying hay. Memories, unbidden and unwanted, whirled up. Those when he was a boy, standing on the floor of the tractor between his father's knees, while his dad drove the tractor through the fields, cutting hay beneath the summer sun.

"When you're a grown man, this will all be yours, son." His father's voice, even in memory, was something he hadn't let himself hear in a long time.

He closed off the memory, but it didn't stop it. His father's voice, the hot rush of summer wind, the faint scent of mechanic's grease and hay brought it all back, as clear as that day twenty years ago.

"This land will be yours, son, and I'll teach you how to take care of it. It's a sacred thing, this land God made, and being a farmer is a great responsibility."

A month later, when the second cutting of hay was growing thick and hopeful in the fields, his father hadn't been there to cut and bale it. Brody's family had been laid to rest in the small town's cemetery, and Brody had never seen his father's land again.

The darkness around him strengthened, drawing his attention to the family's house, where the curtains had not yet been drawn against the coming night. He caught a glimpse of Michelle in the kitchen, the phone cradled on her shoulder, as she opened the oven and slid in a pizza, like the one they'd shared for supper. Still talking, looking as graceful and elegant as goodness could be, she shut the door and swept from his sight.

It was as if a string linked his heart to hers. And as she walked away, she drew that string taut, pulling his chest wide open.

What was it about this woman? He'd been on hundreds of assignments. He'd dated women, trying to find The One, but no lady, no matter how beautiful or kind or successful, had a hold on him like this one.

Floodlights blinked on overhead, lighting up the entire concrete pad in front of the three-car garage. Brody whipped his attention away from the house just in time as Pete ambled into sight. There was an unmistakable air of integrity about the man, a hard-working, down-to-business attitude. No, he couldn't picture Mr. Peter James McKaslin aiding and abetting his brother's illegal activities.

"If you follow the wire, I'll check the lead." Pete cast his glance at the house, as if realizing where Brody had been looking and who he'd been looking at. "Know anything about electronics?"

"Some." Brody reached into the engine compartment to separate the mass of wires and got to work. Testing the charge of each. Working methodically and slow, feeling Pete's curious and finally approving gaze.

"You sure know a lot for a drifter on a bike."

"I'm not a drifter on a bike." Brody didn't feel like lying to this man. Carefully saying as much of the truth as possible, he stopped to follow a negative wire back around to its fuse. "I've been gainfully employed for the last ten years back in Virginia."

"Now and then I hear an accent. Got a decent job? Let me guess. As a mechanic?"

"No. You could call it white collar."

Pete considered that. "Had yourself a fancy corner office?"

"It wasn't a corner, but it was good enough. But I've put in my notice. I'm taking time to decide what I want to do next."

"Wise. You made good money in that office?"

"I did." Brody straightened up. "Here's your problem. The fuse the mechanic changed blew again."

"He said it could."

"Have him order in a new chip, he'll know which one. I can fix this with a pass. It'll be enough to get you by."

"Appreciate it, son." Pete nodded, his brows furrowed not with fatigue but with thought. "Good thing you came along when you did. I'd been asking for help, what with my brother makin' things complicated."

"Ah. Hired him to help and he's not showing up?"

"He works when he does show up. But it's the showing up that's the problem." Troubled, Pete swept off his Stetson and mopped his brow. "Storm's about to break. Best start headin' in."

"This'll take me a minute." Brody hauled his knife out of his pocket and bent to work. "How about you? You've been farming a long time, by the looks of it. Have you ever wanted to do anything else?''

''Never. Working the land is what I'm meant to do.'' Pete gazed at the sky where the first bolt of lightning fingered across the leaden sky. '''Course, some days I have to ask the Lord if He ever meant for me to retire. Seeing as He didn't see to send me a son, I'm not sure what I'm to do with all this land. 'Course, I've got some fine sons-in-law, but they're not farmers.''

''Daughters can be farmers.'' Brody noticed how Pete tensed. His hands fisted.

''Seein' as you and Michelle have struck up a friendship, I don't mind tellin' you that she's had a hard time of it, what with the way her last boyfriend treated her.''

So, that's where Pete was going. To warn Brody off his daughter. Another sign of Pete McKaslin's decency. He loved his family and protected them. Brody knifed through the wire and peeled back the coating. ''Some men don't live up to their word.''

''That's the truth. Turns out Rick figured this was a real valuable spread I had. Thought he'd get himself a rich wife, but he thought wrong.''

Brody heard the unspoken warning. He straightened and closed his pocketknife with a click.

''Some people don't know what's important in life. They think the shortcut to easy money is worth anything, no matter what laws they break. It doesn't matter who gets hurt. When the truth is, what's important and valuable on this farm isn't the property, but the family you raised inside that house.'' Brody met Pete's gaze. Stood tall and straight while the older man took his measure.

Finally Pete nodded. "That'll do." He headed toward the house.

Always on the outside looking in, Brody took his time, keeping a close eye on the house. He watched the kitchen window as Michelle greeted her dad with a smile and waltzed out of sight, only to return with a big glass of iced tea.

There she was, tugging at his insides again, as if his heart was still on that string.

What *was* it about her? He didn't know. He only knew this was wrong on many levels. A highly trained, decorated senior agent did not spend his time on a mission watching a woman serve her father a glass of iced tea.

The trouble was, he couldn't look away. His gaze kept drifting back to her, to her gentle smile, her willowy grace and the way she made him feel. As if she were the answer to every question he'd ever had.

His next thought was torn away by the squeak of brakes and the crunch of tires breaking on the gravel. An older red pickup that had seen better days veered around the parked truck and skidded to a stop.

A truck he'd been hoping to see. The same license plate, make and model that was registered to a Michael M. McKaslin, according to the Department of Motor Vehicles.

Brody figured he deserved a demotion for being distracted while undercover. His captain would have his head for this, if he knew. Ashamed, Brody shut the truck's hood to get his first look at his counterfeiter. They had a fuzzy picture of him from a convenience store tape and another from the bank in Bozeman where he had an account, but nothing had prepared Brody for how much the man had changed in the last few months.

His combed black hair had turned salt and pepper. Bags sagged under his bloodshot eyes. His lifestyle was catching up to him, and he had to figure he was here because they'd been tailing him all across Montana. Where there would be no lease, no utility bill, nothing to let the Feds know where he was.

"Hey, who are you and what are you doin' here?" Mick's suspicious gaze slammed hard into his.

Brody could smell the fear. Yeah, Mick was on his guard. The former rodeo rider motorcycling his way through Montana didn't know Mick McKaslin so he had to keep his cover intact. Brody held out his hand, friendly and easygoing. "I'm Brody Gabriel."

"I bet you're Michelle's new beau."

"A friend." Brody had to set aside everything he knew about Mick McKaslin, on the job, at full alert. "Not a boyfriend. Yet."

Mick chuckled, and the suspicion melted away. "Oh, she's a great gal, my little Michelle. And hey, there she is!"

"Uncle Mick!"

Brody stepped back as Michelle raced across the yard and into her uncle's benevolent arms.

After a quick hug, she stepped away, bright and sparkling. "Where have you been? We were starting to worry. I've got pizza hot from the oven. Want some?"

"You know I do, darlin'. Would it be too much trouble?"

"No way. You know I'd do anything for you."

Brody's stomach turned to ice. What did she say? There was no way she meant it literally. No way. He wouldn't believe it. It was an expression, that was all—

"Here's a little something for my favorite niece." Mick reached into his shirt pocket and pulled out a twenty-dollar bill. "You go buy something nice for yourself next time you're in town."

Brody relaxed. The adrenaline quit squirting into his bloodstream. She was innocent, just as he'd believed.

"Oh, Uncle Mick. You can't keep spoiling me like this."

"What else is my namesake for? Now git on up to the house. I'll drag your new beau in with me. Would like a chance to talk with him."

"*Uncle Mick!*" Michelle turned a bright shade of pink. "Brody, don't pay him any attention."

A sudden gust of wind lifted a dust devil from the driveway and preceded another flash of lightning that seared the sky and seemed to make the ground crackle at their feet.

"It's time to head for cover." Mick whipped off his cowboy hat, gazed up at the sky and then looked straight at Brody. "You can never tell how safe you are. It's always best to be cautious."

An unsettling feeling slid into Brody's stomach. He followed Mick toward the house, glad he had his revolver tucked in his boot. He was determined to banish every thought of Michelle from his mind tonight.

Mick was right. A man could never be too careful.

Zero. It's the last word Brody spelled during their Scrabble match. It was also a number she needed to pay attention to. She had to be losing her mind, because all common sense told her to look the other way when Brody stalked into the room, a predator in black boots and denim, but what did she do?

Look right at him.

He was ignoring her. Following Uncle Mick to the table where her father was rifling through the morning paper he hadn't had time to read. Brody straddled a chair, the way the tough macho heroes did in Western movies, and she felt the knot of emotion harden into an aching ball.

He was a little older than she was. He was well traveled, wiser, worldly and tough. His hands were marked with scars from old cuts—probably rodeo injuries.

She set two empty glasses on the table and filled

them from the iced tea pitcher. Brody didn't look up; he merely nodded his thanks.

Disappointment twisted around her, like a lasso yanking her so tight she couldn't breathe. Yep, he was fully aware of her crush. Of every word she'd created on the Scrabble board because romance had been on her mind. And what had he written?

Loner. Freedom. Single.

Yeah, she got the clue. Michelle left the pitcher on the table. "Dad, I'm going out to put up the horses."

"Thanks, sweetie." Her father answered absently, the way he did when he was preoccupied.

"Can I see the classifieds, sir?" Brody asked in that intimate wonderful baritone of his.

Hearing his voice made her long a little more.

She headed outside, where rain wet her face and washed away her tears.

Chapter Seven

Michelle burst into the kitchen and startled her mom, who turned from the cutting board. "Good morning, sweetie. Where are you off to in such a hurry?"

"Town. I'm meeting Jenna at the diner for breakfast."

"Make sure you eat a well-balanced meal, now." Smiling her approval, her mom returned to dicing potatoes for the frying pan. "Will you be here for supper? Kendra's coming."

"Oh, I've got a late appointment at the Snip & Style, and then I'm going to do Jenna's hair."

"Dear, I guess I won't see you until bedtime. You call me if you're not home by ten, you hear? A mother worries. Oh, and did you hear the good news?"

Michelle stole a raw slice of potato from the pile on the counter. Its sweet crispness exploded over her tongue as she chewed. "You mean about Kendra's new foal?"

"No, dear. Although that reminds me, I need to call her. She's bringing potato salad to supper today. I need her to bring dessert, too. Anyway," Alice continued, as she returned to her slicing, "Uncle Mick's going to buy us out."

"What?" Michelle's keys tumbled from her fingers and crashed on the linoleum at her feet. She knelt to retrieve them, but the shaking didn't stop. Sell the land? Dad was selling the land? Her stomach twisted into knots. "When did you all decide this?"

"Your father's been looking to retire for some time, you know that."

"Sure, but—" Michelle bit her bottom lip before her thoughts could escape. "You'd let Uncle Mick have this place?"

"Your father wouldn't take a contract on the land, Mick's offered us cash. Of course, that doesn't include the twenty acres the house and stables are sitting on. We'd be staying here, so don't look so alarmed, sweetheart."

Michelle's head was spinning.

Sell the land? How could they have done something so drastic without even mentioning it? Her feet felt unsteady as she headed toward the door. Numb inside, she was on autopilot, turning the knob, pulling open the door, stepping through the threshold. "Are you sure you want to sell?"

"We're seeing the lawyer this week." Her mother sure seemed happy at the news. Done with her chopping, she grabbed a bowl and slid the big heap of diced potatoes into it, using the edge of the knife. "Don't worry. You'll always have a home with us."

Michelle tried hard to smile. This was good news for her parents. They had been tied to the land for so long. And now that their family was raised and they were reaching their retirement years, they would have enough money to do anything they wanted.

This was a lot better for them than if they'd been offered a real estate contract. A cash-out deal was a great opportunity for them.

"You have a good day, okay, Mom? Give me a call if you need me to pick up anything in town for you."

"That's a good girl. I might just have to do that. Goodness, your grandmother and I had the best time last night. Holly Pittman's wedding was such an event, I tell you."

"I'm glad." Michelle managed to make it to the back porch.

Since her knees were quaking, she took it as a sign she ought to sit down. The porch step's boards were rough and weathered, but warm from the sun as she settled onto them.

The sweet morning air breezed over her face like a kiss, and Keno grazing with the other horses in the white fenced paddock lifted his head and whinnied a greeting.

This land was her life. She'd lived here every one

of her twenty-two years. Her childhood was here. She'd thought that her future might be here, too.

A shiny quarter landed on the flagstones at her feet.

Brody strode around the corner. He wore a simple white T-shirt and faded Levi's. "Hey, I'd pay you a penny for your thoughts, but you looked so serious, I figured it would cost me more."

"I *was* deep in thought, but then someone interrupted me." She managed to smile. And tried hard not to think about how he wasn't actually looking at her but at the nail beginning to pop up out of the bottom step.

"Sorry. I'm here to fetch breakfast and paint the final coat on the garage. Is your mom inside?" He stuck his hands in his front pockets as if he didn't know what to do with them.

"Yep." She stared at her fingernail polish that was starting to chip. She'd have to fix that. "I hear you get your bike back today."

"Yep."

That meant he'd be leaving. To each thing there is a season, she knew. The Lord had meant for Brody to cross her path. Surely, He had his reasons. "I hope you have a safe journey. That no more deer leap into your path unexpectedly."

"I appreciate it." He started up the edge of the steps, as far away from her as the banister would allow. "It looks like I might not be leaving yet. You know that ad your father put in the newspaper?"

"For seasonal help?"

"That would be the one. I'm thinking of staying, if your dad will have me."

"There's a reasonable chance of that." When she smiled, he'd never seen anything so lovely.

"I never thanked you for everything you did for me that night when I was hurt. I was lucky I was just banged up. If I'd been really hurt, it was good to know I wouldn't have been lying in the road alone."

"No problem. I'm glad you're all right, Brody. Really. That you're able to go on your way, healthy and all in one piece." She felt her stomach clench, because she knew from her older sister's death how final an accident could be. How precious everyone's time was here.

That she shouldn't waste it pining away for something that wasn't meant to be. "I'm glad I could help out. But why would you want to stay here?"

Did he tell her the truth? Not about the mission, but *his* truth? He hesitated, so that one foot was on the top step beside her. "I'd like to work on a farm again. I've been thinking about getting some land. I have a little pocket money saved up. Listening to your father and uncle last night got me to thinking about wide-open spaces."

"Land." Michelle turned wistful. "I'd like that someday, too, but it's way expensive. So that's why I live at home. Okay, the card debt is another, but that's not the only reason. As exciting as big cities must be, I can't imagine living forever bound by concrete and steel."

"You're happy here."

"It's what I am. A country girl." She bowed her head and shrugged, as if she'd confessed too much.

Why was it that he could see her dreams? Brody knew without asking what she wanted.

He saw it all in an image, as if it were a thought of his own. Horses grazing in all these carefully groomed paddocks, which were empty but for a few animals. Hay and alfalfa in the fields, riding a green tractor over the rolling hills, cutting and baling and praying for good weather.

To know the freedom of the wind, the sun and the land.

"I know what you mean." He cleared the gruffness from his voice. "I guess it's hard to take the country out of the boy. Or the farmer."

"Is that why you're retiring from the rodeo?"

"The best part of my life sometimes feels like it's behind me. I don't know if I'm trying to find my past."

"Or your future?"

"Exactly." How could she know? Brody knew full well he ought to be heading inside; he had work to do.

He couldn't seem to step forward, so he sat beside her. "Some of the best memories I have are of being on the tractor with my dad, held safe on his lap, riding out to check on the livestock. Companionable, just the two of us." He gazed into the distance.

"Guess I want to bring back those memories of my dad. Maybe I'll get lucky and find the right woman to marry, so I'll have a son of my own to take out on the tractor. Guess I'm looking for a new life.''

Michelle could hear the longing in his voice. How amazing they had this in common, too. Her heart squeezed. There it was, that connection again, unseen but tangible. Gazing into his eyes, feeling the warmth of his understanding, she was afraid to move for fear of breaking the fragile bond.

It was as if they were breathing together, and she'd never felt so close to anyone. Not physically, but emotionally. It felt as if a string stretched from her heart to his, like those homemade mittens her mom had made her wear when she was in kindergarten. The kind with a string of yarn sewn from one mitten to the other so they wouldn't get lost in the snow.

''I know what you mean,'' she confessed. ''When I was born, I guess my dad always figured out that after six girls he'd never have a son, so I think I sort of was his. I hung out with him, rode in the tractor and the combine. When I was old enough, I helped bring in the crops. I drive a harvester better than anything else.''

''Judging by the dents in your truck, I sure hope so.'' He tossed her a wink and made her laugh.

''I know. You're like everyone else. As if a dented truck and the 411 on the latest fashion trends is the most that you can expect from me.''

''That's not what I think.''

''It's not?''

Please, Lord, help me find the strength to hold back the truth. Brody knew if he said the words he was thinking, he'd tell her what a good and kind person she was. Wonderful and unique. So fresh and untouched and amazing, different from any woman he'd ever met.

He would tell her that when he was back home in Virginia, in his two-bedroom town house and he closed his eyes on another day of hard work done, he was alone—as he'd been for all his adult life.

He would tell her that when he looked inside his soul, she was what he'd been dreaming of.

He was on a mission. He had a job to do. But not forever, he realized. Soon, he would be free to find a whole new life.

Maybe, he reasoned, dreams could come true.

He didn't say another word as he climbed to his feet and ambled into the house. Leaving her wondering. Yeah, he could feel her wondering.

He was wondering, too.

"You look worse than you did last night, and that was with face paint." Hunter surveyed Brody up and down as he was covered in the shade of a cottonwood grove. They were halfway between town and the McKaslins' ranch. "Looks like they've been working you to death."

"I had to really push hard to get that second coat of paint on the garage before noon." Brody, astride the repaired Ducati, whipped off his helmet and let the puff of breeze from the river cool his hot skin.

"Did you bring up the ad in the paper?"

"I waited until Alice was driving me into town to pick up the bike. She was happy with my work, she didn't see why Pete wouldn't hire me on for a while. It could take some time, judging by the way Mick looked me over." Brody told Hunter about Mick's cash offer for the McKaslins' property.

"He'd cheat his own flesh and blood." Hunter looked disgusted. "That may be one way we'll nail him. He's been lying low."

"Think someone tipped him off?"

"Anything's possible. How's that ankle of yours?"

"I heal quick. The sprain was minor. The bike took the worse damage. It turns out the town mechanic is married to one of the daughters. Zach. He offered to show me some riding trails, if I stay around."

"Sounds like a good opportunity. As close as you can get to the family, the better information we can get."

Brody checked his watch. "I've got to get back. Are we still on for tonight?"

"Midnight." Another night of watching Mick's bungalow. Of lying stomach down on the earth letting the snakes hiss at him. "I'll meet you there."

Brody strapped in the small pack, containing the laptop computer he needed and a few extra gadgets. "Take care, buddy."

After he was back on the two-lane road heading north, he spotted a set of tire marks on the pavement where Michelle had skidded to a stop when he'd wiped out. They'd met right here, he thought, and figured it was a sign that he'd even thought about that moment.

He was getting soft. Tough successful agents didn't get distracted by sappy stuff like that.

What he needed to do was to put all thoughts of her aside until the job was done. Then he could start to wonder if she was his future. If there was a chance…

No, he wouldn't think about it. He'd wait until the case was closed and his loyalties were undivided.

That sounded simple. Right?

Wrong. Brody sat in the front room of the second-story apartment and watched the McKaslin house. He'd picked up groceries at the local store and had a package of frozen pizza pockets picked out for dinner tonight, but right about the time he was going to nuke it, he heard a car door slam in the carport below.

Michelle? He'd missed her all day. He'd finished painting the trim on the garage, and accepted Pete's offer to work the next few weeks, just until the first cutting of hay was in. He'd gotten in a hard afternoon in the fields, where Mick worked with the determination of a man on a pilgrimage.

He was lying low. Had Lars Collins gotten word to Mick before Lars was arrested? It had been quiet, they'd made sure of it, but just in case, Brody made sure his revolver was within reach.

He was a patient man. He knew how to wait. And when to move. He'd earn the family's trust, and Mick's as well.

"You did a good day's work, son," Pete told him on the way in from the fields. "I'm glad to have you working for me."

It felt good to have the man's respect, and Brody thanked him for it.

The sun was setting, and family that had gathered for supper at the McKaslin house were leaving. Maybe he'd just pop his head out the door and see if Michelle had come home without him noticing.

Brody opened the door. Michelle's parking spot was empty. But there was Zach helping his wife into a new SUV. He would have been a friend under different circumstances. Zach looked up and asked how the bike was running. Brody could only compliment the mechanic's work.

"Working for Pete this time of year," Zach told him, "you won't get much time off. Sunday, I'll show you those trails I told you about. Give me a call if you want."

It was an offer of friendship. But he was working. They could not be real friends. Wasn't that too bad? What he did accept was the chance to get closer to all the family members. "I sure will."

He felt horrible as he returned to the silent apartment.

Michelle hadn't come home as twilight lengthened and night stole the last of the shadows from the hills. When Hunter's small rock tapped against the glass window, Brody noticed Michelle's truck still wasn't in her covered parking spot.

"She's in town at the diner eating ice-cream sundaes with a girlfriend," Hunter told him the minute they were away from the house. "Don't think I haven't noticed a change in you. She's a pretty girl, but don't get distracted, man. This is serious business."

"You don't have to tell me." He slung the rifle over his shoulder, shrugging the strap into place. Professional. That was what he was.

Then why was she lurking in the back of his mind? How she'd looked this morning sitting on the porch step, not cheerful and sparkling as she usually was, but quiet. And filled with a longing he could feel. Dreams he could see.

Had the Lord brought him here for a reason? While he was lying belly down in the fields with Night Vision binoculars watching Mick's bungalow, he had time to wonder. Was there a greater reason why he'd met Michelle?

As the hours passed, and her truck's headlights cut a bright path through the night, it was as if the stars flickered more brightly.

He felt the answer deep in his heart. *Yes.*

"He's coming!" Michelle whipped forward, nearly knocking her Bible from the pew beside her. She caught it before it tipped, pulse pounding. She'd figured her mom would invite Brody along, but she'd had to get to the coffee shop early and hadn't been able to know if he was coming for sure.

It had been killing her all morning, wondering if she'd see him today.

He was staying. He didn't have to do that. His bike was fixed, his wounds were healing. He could hop on his snazzy red motorcycle anytime he wanted.

But he wanted to stay.

Sure, because he wanted to work on the land again. She knew he hadn't stayed here for any other reason—like for her. She understood how powerful a dream could be.

If she couldn't have her dream, then maybe Brody could find his. Maybe that was why he'd come into her life. To work on her family's ranch. To find both his past and his future, so that when he left them, he knew what would bring him happiness.

I want that for him, please, Lord, she prayed.

She knew the moment Brody spotted her in the crowded church. She could feel the sharp hook of his gaze on her back. Why was he coming after her? Mom and everyone were on the other side of the church. *That's* why she picked this side, where she could hide with Jenna—they were both short enough that they'd been hard to find behind the Pittman family, who were very tall except for Mrs. Pittman and she always wore a hat.

Michelle had hoped she would be perfectly camouflaged, but no. Her life could not go as smoothly as that.

Jenna twisted around in the pew. "Is that Brody?"

"Don't look right at him!" Then he'd know she'd been talking about him. He'd guess her crush was turning into something much more powerful. What would she do if he knew how she felt?

She was trying not to feel anything.

How was she going to deal with him? She'd be cool. She'd be in control. She would not blush or see the dreams he'd told her about in the early morning light. Dreams so like her own.

Friendly. That's what she'd be.

"Michelle! You didn't say you rescued the most gorgeous guy ever! No wonder you have a thing for him."

"I don't have a thing for him."

"Then can I have a thing for him?"

"Jenna!" Then Michelle realized her friend was teasing. "Go ahead. He's a nice guy."

"Sure, you're just head over heels over him. And why not? He's rad. No, don't deny it. You can't fool me."

"Shhh! He's going to hear you."

"Why not? Maybe you should tell him—"

"No, there's no way he can know. He probably already does—" A black leather boot halted at the end of the row. "Oh, hi, Brody."

Just how much of their conversation had he overheard?

She looked up and saw the dark gleam in his eyes. The questioning crook of his brow left no doubt.

Yep. He'd heard.

Was she ever going to stop humiliating herself around him? "This is my best friend, Jenna. Are you trying to find my parents?"

"No, actually, I was looking for you. It's nice to meet you, Jenna." He offered a polite nod to Jenna and moved into the row. "Michelle, would you scoot over?"

"You're going to sit here and torture me?"

"Sure. Besides, you've got good seats."

"This isn't NFL." She waited for Jenna to shift over, so she could, too, taking her Bible and her purse with her. "Why are you avoiding my folks?"

"I was the topic of conversation at breakfast, when I came by to ask which church they attended. They were arguing with Mick about letting me stay. He's insulted your father hired me."

"I love my uncle, but he's unreliable." It was the nicest thing she could say. "I can't believe they're selling him the farm."

"Your parents are selling?" Jenna sounded shocked.

"No one really knows yet." Michelle's stomach soured at the thought. "At least it stays in the family, I guess, but Mick isn't a hard worker. I just think Dad wants to retire. He's a farmer with no sons to take over."

"He has five daughters," Brody added. "Not one of you wants the land?"

Michelle swallowed and looked down at her Bible. There was a pen mark on the cover and she rubbed at it with the pad of her thumb.

Brody's shoulder bumped against hers and remained a steady pressure of hot steel. "Oh, I see. Your father doesn't know."

"No." She'd never had the nerve to ask him. "How do you know what I want?"

"You're easy to read, I guess."

Oh, so this wasn't the same for him as it was for her. This feeling. The way she'd seen his dreams so clearly as if they were projected in front of her on a big screen TV. What did it mean? How was she supposed to help him?

"Are you sure you don't want to sit with my sisters? Karen said you and Zach have struck up a friendship."

"Friends are good. I need more of those, but I'd rather sit incognito with you."

"Sure, you could *try* to go incognito, but you're going to have to work for it because—"

"Of my good looks?"

"Sadly, no. Because you're not a short man. Slump a little, and no one might notice you behind Mrs. Pittman's hat."

"You've done this before?"

"Gone incognito? Sure. I'm always in one kind of trouble or another."

"Shocking, because you *look* like a law-abiding citizen to me."

"Oh, not that kind of trouble. What kind of person do you think I am?"

The nicest person he'd ever met. "I bet you speed. That's breaking the law." He knew because those two tickets were all he'd found on her record. All paid promptly.

"Both times I was talking on my phone and didn't notice I'd crept over the limit. I haven't done that in an entire ten months. I'm very responsible. And why am I defending myself to you? What about you? What kind of laws do you break?"

"Every one."

That made her cover her mouth with her slender, soft hands to hold back genuine laughter. He liked the sparkles that glittered in her pure blue eyes. The rosy color her cheeks turned, and her sweetness. He felt as if he could talk with her and make her laugh for every day to come.

You know I'm looking for a new life, Father. Since he was already in church, the good Lord felt a little closer. *Is this woman supposed to be my new life?*

The choir chose that moment to begin a sweet harmony of reverence that felt like an answer.

Speechless, Brody felt frozen to the pew. Gentle music filled the air, but even more reverent was his awareness of the woman at his side. The brush of her arm against his sleeve and the faint fragrance of strawberries from her hair. They were breathing together, in and then out, the same rhythm, the same *everything*.

Distance, Brody. Remember your duties. Stay distant. Keep your objectivity.

As worshipers shuffled into place and hurried

down the aisle to join their loved ones, he reached for the hymnal the same moment Michelle did. Their hands touched, and he felt as if the light of the sun warmed him for the first time.

Making him wish. Making him see the future that was to be.

Chapter Eight

Michelle thought of Brody all through the service. She tried to concentrate on Pastor Bill's sermon, but her mind kept drifting off, even when she was trying to stop it. She knew exactly who to blame: the man at her side. Who'd come under friendly terms, and the last thing she wanted to be was his friend. Why else had he bantered with her, not as a man interested in courting her but a man with strict boundaries in place.

Friends. Was that something she could accept?

He was like a hero who stepped out of the movie screen and into her life. A man who seemed to *fit*. He loved horses and Scrabble and wide-open spaces and—

Stop thinking about him! She was in the Lord's house of worship. As if she should be even thinking of a man, even in the most chaste and respectful way.

What she should be doing was filling her mind with pious thoughts. Pondering the deep spiritual significance of the minister's words. *That's* what she should be doing.

One day, when she arrived at the pearly gates, St. Peter was going to shake his head at her in disappointment and say, "You should have been paying attention! There's a demerit section, you know. And that's where you're heading, missy!"

She concentrated on today's chosen passage from Chronicles. "Worship and serve Him with your whole heart and with a willing mind. For the Lord sees every heart…"

And she felt assured the Lord could see hers. He had a plan for her, she had to stop worrying about what was to come. To accept each day the Lord gave her and cherish it. She would do the best she could with this day.

And what about Brody? She couldn't help it. There she was, thinking of him again. He appeared to be the model of respect as he bowed his head for the final prayer.

She did, too, concentrating hard on the minister's words. She was so grateful for every blessing in her life. She wanted the Lord to know that. She wanted Him to know she did her best to follow her faith and live by His word.

And as the service ended and shuffling filled the sanctuary, Brody turned to her. "That was a good service. I sure like your minister."

"He's been here since I was in middle school.

He's like a second father to everyone.'' She felt peace deep within her. Because now she had her answer. She knew what she was going to do about Brody.

She was going to forget that he'd guessed she had a crush on him, and she would trust the Lord's purpose in bringing Brody here. She would be his friend.

Whatever path unfurled from that would be the best one, for it was in the Lord's hands.

''Rick alert!''

Jenna's urgent whisper cut through Michelle's thoughts. She jerked to attention.

Two choices. She could stand here and smile with as much dignity as she could manage, or she could leave. If she got in the aisle far enough ahead of him, then she could avoid him entirely.

That was another problem about living in a town so small, you couldn't hide from anyone. You couldn't hide from the man who'd broken your heart.

Brody had risen, all six feet of him, blocking her only escape. Unless she wanted to take on the rest of the Pittman family at the other end of the bench, who were all busily trying to gather shoes and purses and children, then she was trapped.

Brody was such a gentleman, but he was blocking her only escape by politely waiting for the other worshipers to file down the narrow aisle first.

Michelle leaned close to whisper and inhaled his fragrance. Spicy and manly and, hmm, really nice.

"You don't have to wait. There's an opening. Just push your way out there."

"What's your hurry?"

"I've got places to go, people to see." Old boyfriends to avoid. "Please."

"I guess." He waited until there was a clear opening before stepping into it and stood for Michelle to ease out in front of him.

"Thank you, you are such a good shield!" She sparkled up at him with the kind of gratitude he'd expect to see if he'd saved her life.

Then she pulled her friend to her side. Why was Michelle rushing off with her friend? They were like two impatient salmon swimming upstream, careful not to crowd anyone, but making a clear run for the door.

He followed her. He was on the job, of course it was his duty to observe members of the McKaslin family. Mostly, he wanted to know more about this woman who, he figured, might be the one woman on earth who would always keep him guessing.

Michelle glanced over her shoulder, looking down the aisle, and Brody turned, too. He saw a river of faces he didn't recognize. Was she trying to avoid someone? Who?

She'd slipped away from him. He could just make out the top of her golden head in the crowded vestibule. He muttered, "Excuse me," and tried to keep up with her, but she was out the door before he could step foot near the exit.

Then, when he finally made it into the hot blast

of noontime sun, he saw her, the white eyelet dress swirling around her as she helped an elderly lady down the last of the narrow steps.

"You're a dear, you know that?" the woman said, safely on the walkway and settling back on her cane. "I'm looking forward to my appointment on Tuesday."

"Where we'll make you even more beautiful." Michelle flashed the woman a genuine smile.

And like a bullet to his heart, he felt the shock of it. The finality of it. This woman of quiet country goodness and unshakable kindness was the woman he was going to marry. And why? Because what lay lodged in his heart was no bullet at all, but a love so hard and strong, it felt as if it were made of steel. Unbreakable. Unalterable.

Families surged around him, kids running loose away from family members or back again. Real life, bright in the sunshine and as tangible, was everywhere he looked.

They were the people he'd served so long and hard to protect. Whom he'd made enormous personal sacrifices for. Long, lonely years of hard training, harder work and heartbreaking consequences. Friends he'd buried. Innocence he'd lost. Crimes and horror and death that haunted him. That had changed him.

Soon it would be his turn to pass on the weight of responsibility and live a life like this. Where plans for family barbecues were talked aloud and carried on the wind. Where children laughed, arguing over the window seats, where polished and well-kept cars, be they new or old, ferried away their passengers to homes and restaurants and barbecues.

"What are you doing just standing there?"

He looked down to see Michelle at his side, fingering her long bouncy hair out of her eyes with her slender, sun-browned hand.

Tenderness filled him, sweet and heavy like honey. "Figuring out what I want to do next. I have the afternoon free. The weather's good, and your dad's taking the whole day off."

"You start haying tomorrow?"

"Looking forward to it."

To Michelle's surprise, he did seem excited by the idea. The crick at the corner of his mouth was a grin spreading from one corner to the other, showing even white teeth. His relaxed stance said he was comfortable and happy.

Good. She truly hoped he would find what he was looking for. "I'm free, too. Jenna has a family thing she's roped into going to, but I could use company over at the diner. There's a cheeseburger with my name on it."

"What a coincidence. I think there's a bacon burger waiting for me."

"And the best tartar sauce on the planet. Trust me." Michelle took the first step toward the street, wondering how to do this. She'd never had a friend quite like Brody before. Sure, high school guys who were buddies, but friends?

Brody stalked after her and shortened his stride to

match hers. "The best tartar sauce on the planet? How do you know? Have you ever been out of Montana?"

"Sure. Loads of times. Family vacations." she explained. "You know, the pile in the car, road songs until Dad couldn't take it anymore, are-we-there-yet kind of vacations?"

She dazzled him when she smiled, and he could see it, as though the memory were his own. A carload of kids, parents wondering if they'll survive the trip, while trying not to laugh at the antics of their kids but trying to appear stern at the same time.

It was a hope. A vision of what the best of a family could be. But it wasn't Michelle's past he was seeing.

It was the secret wishes within him. The ones he'd never dared to pull out and examine too closely. It wasn't macho. It wasn't tough. He was used to being alone. And to think there could be a place here for him in her life.

It was more than a prayer answered. It was a prayer answered before it was asked.

He stayed by Michelle's side down the length of the old uneven sidewalk, shaded by trees and watched over by tidy bungalows. Brody made sure his pace matched hers. That he stayed at her side—not one step ahead or one behind—all the way.

"No, I can pay for my own." Michelle began digging into her purse for a five-dollar bill. This was no different than going out with Jenna. Friends split the check, right?

"That doesn't sit right with me." Brody reached past her and tossed a fifty-dollar bill on the counter. "I'm the man. I pay."

"Oh? Well, that sounds awfully bossy of you, *plus,* I don't want to scare you off or something, thinking that makes this a date. I know how commitment shy you male types are."

"Me? I'm not commitment shy." He grabbed the white paper bags the teenager behind the counter thrust at him, along with his change.

Michelle grabbed the drinks. "Where do you want to sit?"

"I'm not sure I want to sit with you. I'm still stinging from that commitment comment."

"Well, Mr. Drifter on a motorcycle, if the shoe fits…"

He put the bags down on the nearest available booth. "You mean the boot, don't you, darlin'?"

Oh, his accent was smooth, and it ought to come with a surgeon general's warning. Dangerous. Can cause weak knees and blurry vision. Michelle dropped to the plastic bench seat.

Brody sat down across from her. "At least during a game of Scrabble men don't spell *bride* and *wedding* and *romance.*"

"You had to bring that up!" Her face felt so hot it had to be glowing. "It's just…"

"I know, the way women think. Married women, single women, elderly women. It was different playing with you, that's all, instead of crusty old buddies of mine that don't often see the softer side of life.'' He took a big bite of his burger. Good and juicy. "Different, but nice.''

Across the table, Michelle took a bite of her cheeseburger and they ate in companionable silence for a while.

"What was that back at the church? You know, when you made me knock down women and children so you could dash out into the aisle and leapfrog over people to the door.''

"You have a knack for exaggeration. There was no pushing or shoving, let alone knocking people down and leapfrogging over them.''

"I swear I saw a few bodies left in the aisle. In the church. Seems like St. Peter would take notice of that.''

"Stop teasing me.'' She flicked a French fry at him. "Behave.''

"I'm being a gentleman. Just sitting here finishing my vitamin B burger.''

"Vitamin B?''

"Bacon. It's an essential daily requirement.'' He grabbed his soda, ripped off the plastic lid and drank deeply from the cup. "Stop lobbing food at me because it isn't going to distract me. Who were you trying to avoid?''

"An old boyfriend. While I know he is one of God's children, he is currently disguised by a very greedy facade. There he is.'' She started, turning her head away as a medium-height, medium-build, blond-haired man approached the counter.

Tan trousers. Tan riding boots. Matching shirt, buttoned up to the collar. A new looking Stetson shaded his face. Standing too straight and talking down to the teenager taking his order.

Brody didn't like him. "He can't be the brightest bulb in the pack if he let you go."

"I let him go." She took another bite of her cheeseburger, pretending as if everything was fine.

It wasn't. Brody could feel the pain inside her as if it were his own. Whatever that man did to her was bad. What kind of man could hurt Michelle? She was the kindest person ever.

Protective anger tore him inside out. But he didn't act on it. He crushed the hamburger wrapper in his fist until it was a small, crumpled ball.

What he ought to do is head back to the ranch. He had files to study on his laptop and surveillance data to analyze. There was always the chance that Alice would invite him over for supper and give him a better opportunity to earn their trust. Not to use them, but to protect them.

That's what a responsible, seasoned senior agent would do.

But that isn't what he wanted to do.

He had to be crazy as he held out his hand. "Ever been on a motorcycle?"

"No." Delight sparkled through her like sunshine through the finest of diamonds.

Flawless and pure and unreachable, that's what she was, and she was *his*.

"Are you saying you'd take me for a spin on your bike?"

"Sure. For the right price." He stood, holding out his hand, palm up, to help her from the seat.

Her palm settled against his, a perfect fit. When she smiled up at him, he saw eternity.

It wasn't like riding a horse at full gallop, not in the least. It was more like flying low, Michelle decided as she clung to Brody's solid back. The pavement swooshed into a black blur whenever she looked down. So she didn't look down.

Did she worry about them crashing? No. Brody felt so in control. Competent. She had no problem trusting him completely. He was just that kind of man. Strong, inside and out. Of will and character. With her arms wrapped around his back, she could *feel* it in him.

She'd never met a man like Brody. He was perfect, like knights of old in their tarnished armor, strong and gallant and wise. She longed to lay her cheek against the hard plane of his shoulder blade and just hold on to his goodness and strength.

Of course, the helmet he'd made her wear prevented that. Plus she'd be acting like a forward schoolgirl with a crush and then he would know for sure that she wanted so much more than the friendship she was destined to have with him.

All very good reasons, but they couldn't stop the

longing inside her. *I wish he loved me. More than anything. I wish he wanted me forever.*

Some things weren't meant to be. She accepted that. But deep in her heart she would always love him. Always.

She was grown up enough to accept the Lord's wisdom in guiding her life. Some things weren't meant to be for a greater reason. She believed that the Lord would take both her and Brody on the best paths for each of their lives.

Sure, it would be separate paths, but for now, for His reasons, their paths had crossed. And she would enjoy this rare time with Brody while she had the chance.

Wasn't every moment in this life a gift? Every loved one a great blessing?

Brody was one of those wonderful gifts, and she savored the minutes that sped by like water through a sieve—so fast that she hardly had time to cherish the closeness of being with him. Of holding him tight before he took the last exit off the freeway at the mountain pass and circled back.

As they rode beneath the cheerful blaze of the summer sun toward home, she fought a heavy sadness that grew with each mile. When the ride ended, she would have to let him go.

Brody hated the sight of the McKaslins' driveway, marked by the well-groomed gravel turnout and the red barn mailbox planted neatly to one side.

He downshifted, kicked out his foot to keep the

bike well balanced as he made the sharp turn. He felt Michelle's arms tighten on his shoulders.

On the return trip, she'd been inch by inch loosening her hold on him. He missed the warm band of her arms wrapped around his back. Tenderness burned within him, sharp and aching.

He'd never known any emotion like this. Made of respect and awe and wonder. It felt more powerful than any physical force on earth—and it was inside him. A fierce devoted love that felt as if it were in the very center of every cell and the very essence of his soul.

The McKaslins' two-story house came into sight amid the green fields and rolling hills. He saw a familiar SUV in the driveway and another motorcycle parked next to it. A man was taking off a helmet—Zach. He was a little early for their agreed upon time. Brody hated having to say goodbye to Michelle even five minutes sooner than he had to.

He stopped the bike. Killed the engine. Felt Michelle's hands lift away from the curve of his shoulders. Moving away from him. Taking a part of him with her.

"That was fantastic!" She whisked off his helmet and shook her hair so that silken strands breezed against his arm. "I want one of those, but Dad would put his foot down."

"So hard, it would make a tunnel to China." Zach walked up, swinging his helmet by the chin straps. "I see you've had Michelle as a tour guide. Maybe you don't need me. I could always head on home.

Karen's got everything set up for a get-together tonight. Brody, you're invited, by the way."

"Hey, thanks." He'd like that. But did that mean
he wouldn't get to spend the evening with Michelle?
Or was she part of the get together?

"I'm bringing my Monopoly board. Ooh! I have
to remember to call Karen and tell her." As if in
answer to his unspoken question, Michelle let him
steady her as she climbed off the bike.

A surge of love washed over him as he enfolded
her hand in his. How could he hold back this powerful tide within his heart?

Unaware of his feelings, Michelle flashed him a
smile, the kind that came from not just surface
beauty, but from within. "I had the best time, Brody.
Thanks. I'll remember this always."

"Me, too." I love you, he wanted to say. But how
could he? They weren't alone. He was on assignment. And she appeared to have no obvious feelings
for him.

He thought of something less revealing to say to
her instead. "This sure is some beautiful country
here. The more I see of it, the more I can't believe
my eyes."

"That's how we all feel." She finger combed her
tangled hair with her free hand and spun away, with
as much energy as a young filly, all legs and lean
lines and spirit. "Oh, here's your helmet. Like I need
it in the house."

"You never know. A falling meteor might crash
through the roof. A sudden tornado might roll by."

"It's a clear sky." She brought with her the scent of strawberries and goodness as she handed him his headgear. "I won't hold you up. I know you two handsome dudes have hills to conquer. Trails to blaze. See ya later!"

"Later." Brody revved his bike, cutting off the sound of his voice, keeping his emotions private.

He waited until she'd skipped up the steps and disappeared inside the house before he released the accelerator and the engine quieted down to a low rumble.

"So that's why you're sticking around." Zach was buckling his helmet's chin strap. "You're sweet on Michelle."

"Sweet on her? Nah." That was only the truth. He was to the marrow of his bones in love with her. "I'm just short of cash, and working for Pete seemed like a good idea."

"Sure it is." Zach's chuckle was warm, not censuring. "I could always use another brother-in-law. And before you deny it, I saw the way you were looking at her. A man only has that expression on his face when he means business. She's a real nice person. She'd make a good man a fine wife."

"I know. I'm not out to hurt her, if that's what this is about." His resolve was steel. He loved her. He would never hurt her. He'd die first.

"I'm not worried. You're more than you seem, Brody. I like that. C'mon. I'll show you some of the best trails you've ever ridden."

Already missing Michelle, Brody turned his bike

away from the house and followed Zach's dust trail down the dirt service road that spliced the ranch in two.

He might have left her behind, but his thoughts remained faithfully on her. As they would be for the rest of his life.

He was here on false pretenses. That was the problem. So, how was he going to make her believe his heart was true?

Well, he *was* one of the best agents in his division for a reason. He was capable. He was determined.

He'd find a way to make her believe in his love, with the Lord's help.

Chapter Nine

Michelle tapped along the new cement driveway and up the walk to the front steps of the brick front two-story house and rapped on the glass panel of the screen door. She didn't want to ring the bell in case baby Allie was asleep.

There was no answer, so she juggled the grocery bags and the huge straw bag she'd thrown all her stuff in, and opened the door. "Karen?"

She heard footsteps overhead and sure enough, there was Karen popping around the corner newel post on the landing. "Thanks for not ringing. I just put Allie down. She's actually *sleeping*."

"Oh, that means I have to wait to snuggle her." Michelle laid her bag and sacks on the breakfast bar. "I picked up dessert. Look. Whipped cream. Ice cream."

"I've got syrups and sprinkles." Karen whizzed past her, balancing a laundry basket on one hip, and opened the laundry room door. "When Zach gets back, we'll barbecue. He was glad to have someone to go trail biking with."

"Oh, so he told you about Brody?" *Act cool, Michelle. Chill.* There was no reason to let everyone know about her crush on Brody. She piled the container of Neapolitan ice cream into the freezer as if finding enough space on the wire racks was what really mattered. "I guess he's working for Dad or something."

Karen set the basket down on top of the washer with a thunk. "I guess so. Mom pointed him out to me in church. Sitting right next to you."

Remember, be calm. "He's only a friend. I hardly know him."

"Mom made it sound as if you'd saved his life when he'd crashed on the road, avoiding a mother deer and her fawn." Karen cast a sideways glance, like a detective after the truth.

No way! Michelle thought of Bart, the neighboring farmer who kept trying to ask her out. Maybe a mental picture of him would help. "He got scraped up and hurt his ankle. He's fine. He was nowhere near death."

"Mom sings his praises."

"Oh, really? I guess he's nice enough." Michelle closed the freezer door and wadded up the plastic grocery sacks for Karen's reuse container under the sink. "Did you want me to set up the game?"

"Sure. Kirby called. She's on her way. Kendra

should be here any minute—'' A light rap rattled on the screen door. ''There she is now.''

As Karen rushed off to let Kendra in and inform her of the sleeping baby, Michelle felt horrible. It was the first time she'd ever been dishonest with her sister. She hadn't meant to lie. She'd only been trying to protect her heart.

And why? It was already too late. She'd never had a chance with Brody. She never would. He was...*Brody*. Everything she'd ever dreamed a man should be.

They were friends, that was all. In that, she'd told Karen the truth. As hard as it was, Michelle accepted it. Brody treated her like a friend. He could have taken that friendship to a new level this afternoon, on their trip together.

But he hadn't. No. She knew he never would.

Setting aside her disappointment, Michelle greeted her sister and concentrated on unpacking the game.

Michelle tried to pay attention as Kirby rolled the dice across the crowded board.

''Ha!'' Karen's cry of victory echoed in the high ceilings of the kitchen nook. She'd apparently already counted ahead and was consulting her property deeds for the amount of rent due, even though Kirby hadn't moved her token yet and Allie was yawning, just awake, on her lap. ''Let's see, since I own all three properties and I have houses, you owe me seven hundred and fifty dollars.''

"I'm going to go broke!" With a good-natured laugh, Kirby counted out her play money, handing over one butter-colored hundred bill after another. "Michelle, want to partner up with me?"

"No, I want to win, thank you very much." Her sisterly teasing made everyone laugh and neatly covered up the fact that her thoughts had drifted off to Brody. Again.

Kendra stole the dice, rolled and gave a victorious "All right! Ventnor Avenue. I'll buy it," she said of the last few available properties.

The image of Brody, powering the motorcycle over the lush grass hills flashed into Michelle's mind. Even though he'd been riding away from her...

"Earth to Michelle!" Karen thumbed through the property deeds and tossed the one marked in yellow across the board to Kendra. "I don't think she's paying attention. I wonder where her thoughts could be?"

"And on whom?" Kirby asked, as if she already knew the answer.

"I was wondering if I should buy more houses." Okay, that was a lie; the second one she'd told in two hours! Horribly guilty, she grabbed her assortment of deeds and thumbed through them. Now she would have to think about what to buy to make an honest woman of herself.

Kendra gathered up the dice and slid them across the Free Parking square to Michelle. "I don't know. I haven't met the man, and I know Mom and Dad are singing his praises, but that Brody looks like trouble to me.''

''That's what we like about him,'' Kirby added.

''Not *that* kind of trouble. The bad kind.'' Kendra refused to budge on her opinion. ''I just think Michelle should be careful.''

''Why should I be careful?'' Michelle grabbed hold of the dice and shook.

She let go of the dice and they somersaulted across the board and into one of Karen's hotels. She hadn't breathed a word to anyone how she really felt. But if they already suspected she had a major-league crush on the guy, then how could she act as if he were no big deal? If she admitted it, then she'd never hear the end of the teasing from Karen and Kirby and the scolding from Kendra, who was very suspicious of men in general.

''Brody is just some guy Dad hired to help with the haying, right? No big deal.''

''You just keep telling yourself that,'' Kirby told her.

''Uncle Mick doesn't like him,'' Kendra added.

No big deal. Just keep saying it over and over again, Michelle. Brody Gabriel was just an average, ordinary, no-big-deal kind of guy.

Wrong, her conscience reminded her. *Everything* about Brody was a big deal. The palm of her hand, when he'd helped her off the bike, still tingled from his touch, as if he'd left stardust there to shimmer with a warm glow.

She wasn't going to pretend that she hadn't had a

wonderful afternoon with him. She had. Did she hope for more? Yes. Did she expect more? No.

Sure, he'd charmed her today with his humor and his gentlemanlike behavior. It was probably easy for a man of the world like him, who'd traveled all through the south and southwest, and probably most of the country, rodeoing and probably winning one championship after another, to know what to say to a sheltered, small-town girl.

The fact that she was in love with him wouldn't matter when it came time for him to fire up his polished red motorcycle and ride away forever.

She looked up at the sound of giggling. Kirby was moving the little silver shoe, Michelle's token, all seven squares according to the number indicated by the dice.

"No, she doesn't like Brody at all," Karen commented wryly.

Michelle's face turned hot. She'd been caught. Okay, so she was a terrible actress. But she was trying to keep her head on straight, thank you very much, and that wasn't always easy.

Kendra consulted her deeds. "Michelle, you owe me seventy bucks."

Michelle blinked. "How much?"

"I'll just take it." Kendra tugged a fifty and a twenty out from where Michelle had tucked them beneath the edge of the board. "You're in big trouble if you're that far gone on him."

Michelle knew her face had to be bright red. Her skin felt hot enough to cook eggs on. "Can't we change the subject? What about Uncle Mick buying out Mom and Dad?''

''I don't know. Uncle Mick is great and everything, and he's always been good to us, but he's declared bankruptcy twice.'' Karen searched for the dice. ''I'm afraid he'll let Dad down. What if he breaks up the land and sells it off to development?''

''That's the kind of thing he'd do,'' Kendra agreed. ''He's always looking for easy money.''

At least that worked, although the new topic wasn't any better. She loved her uncle. They all did. He was fun and sent great presents and always doted on them. But he had problems, just like anyone else. A lot of them.

''At least Dad's making Uncle Mick work this time.'' Karen rolled the dice. ''Of course, he had to hire Brody to pick up the slack.''

Kendra looked troubled. ''Mick's not pulling his fair share *and* he's moved into the bungalow rent free. It's hurting Dad. What if Brody is just another man cut from the same cloth Mick is?''

''He's not. I *know* it.'' Michelle bit her tongue. Had she really said that? Had she really leaped to his defense with that much oomph?

Across the table, Kirby sparkled with delight. ''I saw him in church, too. Of course he was hard to see behind Mrs. Pittman's impressive hat. He's not a bad-looking man. Not as handsome as my Sam, but then, who could be?''

''Or my Zach,'' Karen agreed. ''But Michelle's Brody is a close third. What do you think, Kendra?''

"He's not my Brody!" Michelle protested. This was why she didn't want them to know!

"His looks may be all that he has going for him, but Dad did say he was a hard worker," Kendra conceded. "Still, it takes a long time to know a person. People have many layers. Everyone has things they don't want you to see."

"That's not necessarily a bad thing," Kirby added.

Pain flashed in Kendra's eyes from past experience, and Michelle guessed that whatever had happened to her sister wasn't something she ever talked about. It had been something that changed her opinion of men forever.

Kendra stood her ground. "Look at Rick. We all thought he was a good guy, but he was lying to Michelle. To all of us."

It hurt to remember how gullible she'd been. How much she'd trusted him. But what else should she have done? Approach the potentially most important relationship in her adult life with suspicion and a closed heart?

"Take your time if you're interested in this man, this Brody," Kendra advised. "Promise me. There's no hurry to fall in love. No hurry to trust someone until you're sure they deserve it."

"Love?" Karen's mouth dropped open and she searched the board for her token.

"I didn't say I was in love with him!" Michelle tipped over her iced tea.

Kendra jumped up with a napkin and came to the rescue. "Awfully defensive, aren't you?"

"No! I'm not in love with him!"

"Yes, you are. Ooh, it sounds like my husband is back from his ride." Karen looked up at the sound of a motorcycle pulling into her driveway and seemed to remember she had a hold of her token, and so she moved it. "Not so good. I'm in jail."

"Yeah, you derelict." Michelle had enough talking about Brody so she bounced out of her chair and wanted possession of her niece. "Allie can't stay in jail with you. She did nothing wrong."

"Not Allie, the most perfect baby ever," Karen agreed as she lifted her infant with one hand on her bottom into Michelle's waiting arms. "Perfect timing. She needs changing."

"Fine. That's the price I pay to get away from you guys and all your gossiping and making up wild stories about me." Michelle cuddled Allie, who promptly grabbed a handful of Michelle's hair and pulled.

"We're not imagining the blush on your face," Kirby called out. "Karen, you get to roll again."

"I'm not blushing!" Michelle said it with enough force, hoping it would make the heat on her cheeks fade. Of course it didn't. She cradled Allie close as she made her escape while she could. "And I'm not in love with him," she called over her shoulder, just to have the last word.

Did it work? No.

"Are you at least *starting* to fall in love with him?" Karen asked.

"No!" Her denial echoed in the stairwell as she started up the carpeted steps to the second story.

"Liar!" Kirby accused.

"Okay, I admit it. Just don't tell anyone else." Michelle paused on the landing where she could just see her sisters at the kitchen table around the polished newel post. "*Maybe* I've got a little bit of a crush on Brody. Okay, a *huge* crush."

She hadn't taken two steps before she heard the screen door rasp open and a man's boots hit the wood floor. Did Zach hear what she'd said? Her face flamed again. How could he have missed it? The back door had been open.

Then a second set of boots struck the kitchen floor. A tingle crawled along the back of her neck. Brody? *Please, Lord, don't let that be—*

"Hi, Brody."

"It's Brody."

Her sisters sounded way too pleased.

He'd had to have heard what she'd said. Ready to die, Michelle hugged Allie harder, glad her beautiful little niece was giving her an excuse to never go downstairs again.

"Root beer or cola?" Zach asked from behind the open refrigerator door.

Brody tried to force his stunned mind to function. Michelle's words were still ringing in his head.

Maybe I've got a little bit of a crush on Brody. Okay, a huge crush.

She did?

He felt the weight of three women, Michelle's older sisters, watching him and wondering. He might be a seasoned agent, trained to handle any situation, but he wasn't prepared for this. For two women smiling at him like he was the best joke they'd ever seen, and the third looking at him as if she expected him to have a rap sheet twenty pages long.

"Uh, root beer." He was relieved when Zach handed him a cold can over the top of the refrigerator door.

He almost dropped the can. His fingers didn't work. What was with him? All he could think about was Michelle's voice replaying in his head like a recording. *A* huge *crush*.

He could see his new friend's amused response as he took a soda for himself and shut the door. Zach seemed amused but not accusing, as if they were only two men and outnumbered, so they had to stick together.

"Hey, Brody." Zach gestured with the liter bottle of soda he carried to the round table where Michelle's sisters were watching him over their Monopoly board. "Meet the rest of the gang. This incredible lady is my wife, Karen. Kendra is the horse lover of the family, and that's saying something. Kirby, here, is the sister we pretend we don't know."

"Yeah, I'm out on five different warrants. It's shameful."

"Says the quietest one of all," Zach interjected. "Would any of you ladies like a refill?"

"Such service. Thank you, handsome." Karen rewarded her husband with a sweet and affectionate kiss.

Brody popped the top of the can and sucked down a couple gulps of soda. The fizzy sweetness wasn't enough to wash away the ache of emotion in his throat. This nice new home with the roomy kitchen and large bay window eating area, with its warmth and simple charm and framed pictures of family on the walls. It was a house filled with love.

It amazed him that families existed like this. So one family was raised in love, and now those daughters were making homes and families of their own. Little baby things were everywhere. A swing in the family room by the sofa. A scattering of toys on the floor. It was like something out of TV.

It was new to someone who'd been alone for all his adult life. The man in him ached for what these people had. Family. Love. Friendship. The agent in him acknowledged they weren't criminals. He didn't need more surveillance to know it.

"C'mon and join us," Kirby invited as she started collecting up the colorful play money. "We'll start over. Everyone was about to lose to me anyway. You guys come join us."

"I'll pop corn," Zach volunteered as he added soda to the rest of the glasses on the table. "Kirby, give Sam a call. See if he's done at the airfield. What do you say?''

A round of feminine ''yeahs'' filled the room, and the warmth and coziness left Brody spinning.

An evening of Monopoly? He'd done a lot in his line of work. He'd lain on his stomach in mud and rain in the cold foothills of the Cascade Mountains surveilling an extremist group gone bad. That hadn't been pleasant.

He'd been in shoot-outs and riots. And there was the time he spent three months in east L.A. as a homeless man. That had been a tough assignment. He'd handled escaped felons, drug dealers, gang members and murderers, but never something like this.

Television shows were made of this. Not experiences in his life.

He ached with a need he couldn't name. A need he'd never paid attention to before. It overwhelmed him as everyone in the kitchen watched him expectantly.

''Sure.'' He shrugged in agreement. ''A game of Monopoly won't kill me.''

''No,'' Karen agreed, ''but Michelle might kill *you*, Kirby, when she realizes you invited Brody to stay after—'' She lifted her brows suggestively.

Michelle's words played through his mind again. *I've got a little bit of a crush.*

It blew him away. Michelle had feelings for him? He wanted to shout so everyone would know how incredible that felt. How impossible.

He couldn't—and not because it would make him

look like a nut. He was on assignment—undercover, with the objective to observe the family and gather evidence to either indict them or clear them. Tonight would be an agent's dream of infiltration. They'd extended an invitation and their trust.

But there was nothing typical about this assignment or this family or this girl. No, Michelle was amazing. One of a kind. Even though she'd left the room, he could feel the echo of her heartbeat between his own. He could feel a tug of connection like an unseen string binding them together.

He felt alive for the first time in his adult life.

These feelings were new and they weren't because he'd been alone for nearly two decades. Or because he'd lost his family long ago. He knew these feelings weren't because the years since had been solitary and colorless, like a black-and-white photo with no vibrancy and no life.

He felt this way because of Michelle.

Zach brought in two chairs from the dining room table, and Brody moved to help him. Karen scooted her chair over so there was room for him right next to Michelle. The tall, silent sister, what was her name? Kendra, glared at him with warning in her eyes. He couldn't blame her. In a good family, a big sister looked out for her little sister.

"Which token do you want?" Kirby asked him as the sisters handily restocked the money and turned in the houses and hotels and property deeds. "Michelle always takes the shoe."

"Doesn't matter." He didn't care. He hadn't played Monopoly since he was a boy.

Kirby picked the top hat for him before she tossed the car at Zach.

Everybody seemed used to the routine. Zach began popping the corn. Kendra gathered up the houses and hotels. Kirby divided the play money by color.

What should he do?

Karen leaned close. "Someone's going to have to tell Michelle to come down. I could do it, but she's going to resist my best efforts. If I know Michelle, she'll find a way to stay up there forever. She's a little embarrassed."

All eyes turned to him, and Brody could feel their amusement. And their expectations.

"Go on up," Kirby urged with a wink.

Don't you do it, the seasonal agent in him ordered. There was no sense spending more time with Michelle. Not until he could close this case and come to her a free man, his work done.

But the man in him, who'd been alone for too long and saw an end to it, couldn't help it. He looked in the direction of the stairs and along the polished wood banister leading up and out of sight. If he followed that path, would it change his future?

He had evidence to find. A case to investigate. The Bureau depended on him to do his job and do it well. And to do that, he had to stay focused.

It wasn't his loneliness, he realized, that he felt so keenly here among this loving extended family. It was something greater. Something as powerful as gravity that kept the planets in alignment around the sun and the stars in place in the galaxy, and the power of it lit up his soul. Made him see what he'd been fighting so hard to ignore. For like gravity holding the moon to the earth, and the earth to the sun, so his soul was bound to Michelle's.

He set his soda can on the table and his feet led him to the stairs. Inexorably, it felt as if every moment in his life had happened for the sole purpose of bringing him here. To this place and time.

He took the first step and the next, rising up to the second story, where Michelle was. He wasn't sure his boots were touching the carpet.

Fear gathered in the pit of his stomach. He felt numb. He felt as if the love that bound them was pulling him forward, like a boat in a strong current. This was a different kind of fear than he'd known before. He was used to shoot-outs and takedowns and violent criminals. Life and death situations.

As he followed the low murmur of Michelle's voice, he felt abject terror. There was more than his life at stake. It was his future. It was his soul.

The murmur became music and he waited outside the doorway. Just looking at her. She was enough to fill his senses and his heart for eternity.

He'd never seen any woman look so beautiful. Sunshine slatted through the blinds in the big window seat behind her, cherishing her as she sat in a wooden rocker holding her precious niece. She gazed down at the infant while she sang a lullaby he didn't recognize, singing the melody so quietly, he couldn't hear the words. The gentle grace wrapped around his heart and held him captive. Opened him wide.

All he was, all he would ever be was hers. It wasn't a decision.

It just was.

As if the angels had brought him here to find the woman he was destined to love for all time.

"She's asleep," Michelle whispered to him without looking up, changing to a soft hum as she stood with her lithe elegance and carried the child to her crib.

He watched captivated as Michelle gently laid her beloved niece in the polished and well-appointed crib. Love shone in this room from the coordinated wallpaper and window coverings to the mobile and sheets. Love shone, too, on Michelle's face and in every gesture as she brushed her hand over the infant's soft blond head.

She'd make a great mom. Brody had never let his thoughts wander in that direction before. No woman had ever inspired that thought in him until this moment.

"What are you doing up here?" She didn't look at him as she stepped into the hall and she drew the door nearly closed behind her.

"I was sent up to fetch you. They're starting a new game and they're waiting for you."

"No, I mean, what are *you* doing here? In my sister's house?" She deliberately moved in front of him so that she didn't have to look at him. Because then she'd see the horror on his face. She'd see the rejection. Because he *had* to have heard her. Had to have overheard her confession.

"Zach invited me, remember?"

Great. She just knew who to thank for her humiliation. Michelle walked fast as she could down the hall, but Brody kept a pace behind her.

Thank heavens he wasn't going to bring up what he'd overheard. He wasn't going to make an issue of it. Okay, so she was clued in. There was no way that a great guy like him with the world at his feet was going to fall in love with a small-town girl like her.

So what did she do now? She felt unsteady, so she grabbed the banister railing for support. The wood was cool and smooth beneath her hand as she kept ahead of him so that it didn't feel as if they were going down the stairs together.

She took one look at her sisters, all smiling and happy for her—except Kendra, who never thought falling in love was a good idea. Even Zach was beaming. There was a rap on the screen door and through the mesh she could see Kirby's husband, Sam, a big hulk of a man, flash her a knowing wink.

They all thought it was so cute, the way she had a crush on Brody. She did *not* think it was cute. At all. Not when everyone knew about it.

"We've saved your place, Michelle." Karen gestured to two empty seats beside her. "And one for Brody. We decided to seat you two together."

Wasn't that special? Oh, this was going to be so

uncomfortable! Could anything be more embarrassing than this? She didn't think so. Everyone acted as if Brody had proposed, and how crazy was that?

Well, *he* was acting as if nothing had happened. Good call. That's exactly what she was going to do, too. Just erase that comment she made so she could pretend it never happened. Hit the delete key. Press the back button and rerecord. Erase the chalk from the blackboard.

She dropped into her chair as Zach rescued a popping bag from the microwave. Sam took a seat next to Kirby, Kendra got up to get napkins, Karen asked about Allie, and through all the activity, as loud as it was, it was merely background noise to the fact that Brody was easing into the chair beside her.

Love filled her. Gentle and sweet and life changing, making her all shivery and tingly and lifting her up, as if she were sitting on a big fluffy cloud.

She was only distantly aware of Zach setting two popcorn bowls on the table. The buttery good fragrance might be one of her most favorite on earth, but not even popcorn could tear her attention away from Brody. His iron-hard arm brushed hers.

A place in her heart opened. A place she'd never known before. And it filled with a love so pure and great, she felt as if it changed her. Completed her.

"Michelle, it's your turn." Kendra nudged her. "Stop daydreaming and roll."

"Daydreaming?" She hadn't been daydreaming. This was no dream. This was real, and she was full and floating. She hadn't even got to dreaming yet.

She grabbed the dice and rolled, barely paying attention as Brody took the dice next and rolled. Did she notice what happened next? No. She was only aware of his scent, the rhythm of his breath, the brush of his skin to hers, the shift of his body, the beat of his heart within hers. The overwhelming love that left her dazed.

Kirby's husband, Sam, rolled high and started the game. She heard the tumble of the dice on the board and the groans as he dropped his token on a property.

"I'll buy. The railroads always bring me luck." Sam slapped his money down in front of Kendra, who was in charge of the bank.

Kendra separated the play bills. "Michelle, you're in charge of the properties."

"I am?" She hadn't even noticed the stack of cards someone had placed right in front of her.

Somehow she thumbed through the cards. Luckily, someone had put them in order and she didn't have to go far to recognize the deed. "Sure, like you got the first railroad, but I'm going to get the other three."

"That's what you think, kiddo," Sam threatened with a teasing wink.

"Is that a challenge?"

"More like a declaration of intent."

Kendra rolled and the dice tumbled across the board and into a tumbler of soda. She squealed when she got doubles. She moved her token onto Vermont

Avenue. "I'll buy, and I get to roll again. Okay, dice. I need a seven so I can take the next railroad."

"Kendra, how's the new filly?" Zach asked.

"Shh, I'm trying to concentrate." Kendra cupped the dice, as if to exert her will on them.

Brody felt Michelle's fingers brush his wrist. "Do you think you can stand my family? Are you ready to run for the door?"

"Nah, I'm going to hang around. People who act like this need to be kept under close surveillance. Soda and popcorn and Monopoly. I saw Zach stoke up his grill on the back deck. My guess is barbecued hamburgers."

"Kendra brought the potato salad." When Michelle looked up at him, it was with a new light in her eyes. A radiance that matched the glow he felt inside.

As if a dream inside him had been brought to life. A chance for real love. For a real life. A secret wish he'd been too afraid to pray for all these years. But it had lived inside him all the same. The hope that one day he would find not what he'd lost as a boy, but what he needed as a man to make him happy. What he'd never figured he'd find—a woman of goodness and gold and spirit.

God had planned this all along. Brought him here on his last assignment.

The last thing I can do is fall in love now. In the middle of an investigation. *Please, show me what to do next, Lord.*

It felt more than wrong to be investigating these

people. They were good, kind, decent. A real family with a bond that wrapped around him. Without question. Without judgement. Including him in their good times. Trusting them with their beloved youngest sister.

She sat next to him, spine straight, feigning disappointment when her sister landed on and bought Pennsylvania Railroad. Apparently it was a longstanding family battle for those properties.

"My turn!" She rolled the dice and watched them roll. "No! Oh, no."

She hid her face in her slender hands. Her gold bracelets clicked. Her earrings brushed against the soft skin against her jaw. She was so delicate and feminine and so amazing. He loved her so much that he hurt.

"I can't believe this!" Good-naturedly, Michelle laughed at herself, too, moving her little silver shoe to the Reading Railroad. "I can't believe I owe you, Sam. Yeah, I know, twenty-five bucks."

"Hand it over." Sam seemed like a good guy, holding out his hand for the rent payment. "Hey, too bad this isn't real money."

"Yeah, Michelle, you could pay off your credit cards," Karen piped in. "And buy my half of the coffee shop."

"I don't want to own your coffee shop. I love working there, don't get me wrong, but owning a business just isn't for me." Michelle gathered the dice and pushed it in Brody's direction. "I have other dreams."

Brody didn't mind the way the sisters exchanged questioning looks and amused comments. No. He knew about dreams. Because he was sitting right beside one. A dream, rare and perfect, that God had placed within his reach.

Brody vowed right there and then, as he rolled the dice and landed right next to Michelle on Reading Railroad, that being stuck beside her was exactly where he wanted to be.

For the rest of his life.

Chapter Ten

"This is so like a movie or something," Jenna said, as she loosened the reins to let her horse drink from the creek.

"Definitely a movie," Michelle agreed as she gave Keno his head so he could drink from the cool water, too, on what felt like the hottest day they'd had so far this summer.

It had been exactly a week since she'd spent time with Brody. Between her work schedules, she was gone long hours. It was a peak time for both the salon and the coffee shop. Between people getting their hair done before going on vacation and tourists spotting the coffee shop and stopping by for iced drinks and a bite to eat.

Brody had spent long hours with her dad in the fields. She'd spot him every morning when she fed and watered the horses. He'd be already hard at work, a speck against the distant fields, at her dad's side. She'd come home after dark every evening this week, and Brody's lights had been off in his apartment. Probably sound asleep from the long day of manual labor.

She missed him. It was as simple as that. And today, he hadn't been at church. He hadn't been at his apartment afterward. His bike was missing from its usual place in the carport. Where had he gone? Or maybe—she hated to think it—he'd been trying to avoid her.

The Monopoly game had been fun, with Sam and Kirby teaming up to defeat Karen and Zach. Zach had grilled burgers and they'd eaten on the shaded deck outside, talking about nothing, really. But every moment, Michelle had been aware of what she'd said. Of how he'd overheard her. Of how he didn't react at all.

The first available chance he'd gotten, he probably decided to avoid her. Keep his distance because it was easy to see what she wanted. A man to marry. A man to love. She wanted that man to be him.

"It's too romantic for words." Jenna sighed. "The mysterious stranger comes to town and falls in love with one of the locals. It's a happy ending all around. An idyllic courtship. A heartfelt proposal. A wedding of her dreams. And a husband to die for."

"Heck, why stop there? Let's make him financially well off. And he has to be happy living in a small town."

"And never leave the love of his life again."

It was too good to be real. Michelle knew that. And it hurt. "Keep dreaming, Jenna. Maybe one day it could happen."

"Dreams happen all the time on TV. You just have to know which shows to watch."

Jenna was teasing, sure. But what about real life? Michelle shifted in the saddle at the sound of a motorcycle. It was only a kid on a dirt bike revving along the public trail. Not Brody.

She shouldn't feel so disappointed. "I'm talking real life here. Sure, romance is nice, but do you know what? The problem with romantic dreams is that they involve men."

"They are *supposed* to involve men," Jenna said.

"Yeah, but men are…*men*. You know. Maybe there are fewer good ones than we think."

"I know what this is about." Jenna drew solemn as the horses, having their fill of the cool water, lifted their heads and splashed back to the trail. "This is about Rick."

"No, this is about reality. Good men don't just fall from the sky. Or fall in front of you in the road. There's always a catch." She knew he didn't want her. *That* was the catch.

"Are you saying Brody isn't a good man?"

"He's a great man. I've never met anyone like him." Longing punched inside her. "But I'm not going to let this crush turn into anything else."

It was too late, she knew. But it was her story, and she was sticking with it.

"Because he's like such a mystery? A stranger?

You hardly know anything about him. He just shows up in town. That would make me nervous, too, if it came to risking all my heart.'' Jenna was completely sympathetic, one hundred percent understanding.

Even so, Michelle still couldn't say the words out loud. She loved Brody. If she kept it silent and to herself, then maybe it would hurt less when he broke her heart. ''Mr. Wonderful, Dark and Handsome is going to leave one day. And this time around, I'm going to keep my dignity.''

''This *is* about Rick!'' Jenna sounded so distressed. ''You can't let someone who lied to you influence the rest of your life.''

''I know. I believe that, too. This is about me. If Brody doesn't know how I really feel, he can't hurt me as much.''

''You don't know that. You might have to give him time. You'll get to know him more and maybe he'll get a crush on you.''

''I wish.'' But she wasn't holding her breath. She'd probably faint from lack of oxygen.

The truth was, Rick had shattered her. He'd been her first big love. He'd come with flowers and promises and praises that made her feel cherished and special. She believed him. And when he'd betrayed her, when she found out the kind of man he truly was, she'd felt worthless. She hated to admit it, but she did. She'd let a man who didn't respect her make her feel as if she'd never be good enough.

And how bad was that?

But he was one man. Not Brody. Brody was the

genuine thing. A real man. One who worked hard, lived with integrity, who had never lied to her. Never pretended.

She respected him for that. Admired him even more.

The thought of trusting a man, really trusting him, made her shake down to her soul. But when she thought of Brody, she wasn't as afraid. He was one man worth trusting. She knew it down deep.

That's how much she loved him.

They'd reached the part of the trail where the public river trail bordered her family's property. As they'd done since they were six years old, Michelle drew her horse to a stop at the path that trailed through the alfalfa fields. Her way home. "Did you want to come over and have supper with us? Tonight we're at Kirby's house."

"Nah. I'd love to, but it's my brother's birthday. We're having a dinner over at my gramma's house. I'll call you later?"

"'Kay." As they had done for almost twenty years, Michelle nosed Keno down the path that would take her home, waving a final goodbye to her best friend.

She wasn't going to think of Brody. She wasn't. What she had to do was find a way to keep the love she felt for him locked away and hidden. Her very own secret.

If only he wanted her. If only he loved her. She'd wished for a lot of things in her life, but nothing with as much genuine longing as this.

Nothing had seemed so impossible.

Keno nickered, stalling in the middle of the path. His ears swiveled and he lifted his nose, smelling the sweet-scented breeze. An odd flickering began at the nape of her neck and rose up over the back of her head. Her pulse began to pound not from fear but from recognition.

She stood up in the stirrups and saw the familiar palomino. What was their horse doing tied up out here. And wait, there was something moving in the grass. A shock of dark hair, a hard curve of steely shoulder—

Brody.

"You were right, buddy," Hunter's voice crackled in Brody's ear. "Mick may be lying low, but he can't keep away from the blackjack tables."

"It about killed me today to watch him go and I couldn't tail him." Brody had spent the better part of the afternoon coordinating the operation that kept Mick under surveillance. "Did we get him on the cameras?"

"I'm with the head accountant right now. She came in just to help us. We've got the casino's security cameras watching his every move. He hasn't passed one of his twenties. *Yet.*"

"He will. With the setup I saw today, he'll use the cash. He can always make more."

"You were in his house?"

"Yep. And the captain is going to like what I found." It was exactly what he'd been expecting, but better. Much better. "How's the warrant coming?"

"I've got to check my e-mail. Daggers was going to let me know as soon as he gets it. I'll call you. Hey, and be careful."

"You, too, buddy." Brody clicked off the phone and shoved it into his back pocket.

While he was here, he'd change the battery packs in the hidden surveillance cameras he and Hunter had set up during their after-midnight missions.

The snap of breaking grass made his blood freeze. He'd been keeping an eye the road, and he was pretty well hidden by the crest of the gentle rise of the land. So if someone was sneaking up on him, from the fields rather than the road, he was in trouble.

In a flash he saw it all: his cover blown, Mick stalking him through the grass. Years of training had him reaching instinctively for the revolver tucked in the back of his jeans.

Instinct made him hesitate, too. He didn't draw his weapon. There was *too* much noise. Something felt off. Wrong. There wasn't a threat in the air. The larks were undisturbed, squawking happily. He heard the seed-heavy grasses rustling in the ever-constant breeze and the sudden low, *whoof* as a horse exhaled loudly.

Not the horse he'd saddled up to ride out here, but another one. His horse stood at attention, ears swiveling, nickering a greeting to an approaching horse.

He felt a shock of emotion. Soft and gentle. Without thinking he swung in the direction of the river where he'd noticed a path leading to the public riding trail.

He already knew who was taking a shortcut through the field. He knew because he could feel her. He eased up out of the grasses and spotted the brim of a lady's Stetson, the bounce of a ponytail and her perfect profile. The wink of gold jewelry in the sun.

Michelle. His entire being filled with tenderness. That was the woman he was going to marry. It was the only thought in his mind.

That was wrong. It was dangerous to be this distracted. He couldn't help himself. The cowboy hat she wore was small, just enough to shade her eyes, but not the soft beauty of her face.

"Brody, is that you?" She squinted at him because of the distance. "What are you doing hiding in the grass?"

"I'm up to no good." He swiped the bits of grass and dirt from his jeans and climbed to his feet, thankful the small knapsack he'd carried camouflaged well with the grass and dirt. He'd come back to get it later. "Just out riding and took a break."

"Dad gave you permission to ride Jewel? I can't believe it. *I* don't get to ride his favorite horse. How did you get so lucky?"

"She'd come up to the fence when I was passing by and I petted her. We seemed to strike it off." He gathered the mare's reins and untied them from the low bush he'd tethered her to. "Your dad said I had a way with her, and how hard I've been working for him. So he said since I had the experience to handle her, that I might as well ride her.''

"He's a tough taskmaster, you know."

"He likes a job done right and done well. So do I."

"So *that's* how you won him over." Michelle knew the admiration showed in her voice. Her dad did have high standards, and he liked Brody. That said something about the kind of man Brody was.

"I like your dad." Brody pulled a mint candy from his pocket and let Jewel lap it from his palm. "Pete and I found out we have a lot in common. One is a respect for horses. We started talking, and one thing led to another. I wound up telling him how much experience I've had in the saddle."

From the rodeo, of course, and being around horses growing up. Michelle gave her Keno a pat on the neck, and a "good boy" for standing so patiently.

She swung down, the creak of the leather saddle as familiar as the ground at her feet. The mild wind, scented by the ripe grass and maturing alfalfa in the field, swept over her, as those smells had every summer of her life.

What wasn't familiar was the man striding through the grass to meet her. Even with Jewel's reins in his hand, he moved with the predatory might of a hunting wolf.

Everything about him, from his intense gaze to the indomitable set of his unshaven jaw to the hard bunch of his muscles beneath the denim fabric, made her want to run.

Every time she saw him, there was more to see. More of his strength. His power. His integrity. Like a cornered doe with no out, she tensed—too paralyzed to fight the inevitable. The secret love within her doubled, expanding through her whole being.

Stop gawking at him, Michelle. You can't let love grow for him, remember? He knew she had a crush on him, but he didn't know the truth. He didn't know the depth of what she felt. The force of it.

She needed to act as if he didn't matter. As if they could still be friends. Sure, and exactly how did she do that? It was impossible to shut off the feelings inside her. To deny her heart. Especially when he was striding through the grass with a fiercely intense look on his face.

He was coming after her like a man used to dominating everything around him. Someone who was in control and forged his own path.

That was scary, not because it was threatening, but for a whole different reason. She quaked inside, deep in her spirit, where she was the most vulnerable.

Could she let him know that? There was just no way. "What were you doing out here? Wait. I know. You were keeping the snakes and the flies company."

He didn't crack a smile. "I'm on the lookout for the nosy female who just interrupted my nap."

"Hey! I'm insulted. I'm not nosy."

"Then what are you doing out here?" He looked intimidating, but a spark of trouble glinted in his dark gaze. "Come to spy on me, huh?"

What *was* he up to? "This is my family's land. I was passing by and decided to see what kind of varmints were infesting the field."   .

"No varmints here. Just an upstanding guy out for a little peace and quiet."

"Then I guess I'll just have to leave you here in the grass with the rest of the snakes," she said kiddingly, but that was not how she felt. Not at all.

She wanted to keep the conversation light, but inside she felt as if her sadness weighed a ton. Maybe two tons. Brody wasn't looking at her. He had to be thinking what he had done to deserve a woman's schoolgirl crush?

You captured my heart, that's what.

Maybe she ought to mount up and save what little dignity she had left. "Are you headed back to the house?"

"No destination, really. Just enjoying the day. Well, almost evening." His stony expression softened and he tossed her a sheepish, lopsided grin.

It was devastating. She wanted him to love her. She longed for it with her entire being.

She needed to face the truth: he didn't want her. *Stop doing this to yourself.*

She couldn't help it. Just as she couldn't stop the warm glow of tenderness within her. The most she could do was deny it. She lifted her chin, prayed for strength and the wisdom, and made her decision.

His shadow fell across her, shielding her from the sunlight. Standing before her without saying a word.

What was he thinking? He wasn't mocking her. He wasn't making fun of her. He wasn't running for the hills. Instead, he met her gaze and the impact of it felt like a great intimacy. As if he intended to see everything within her. Every gleam of love. Every burn of adoration.

It was as if there were only the two of them in the entire world. Her vow not to let herself love him any more crumbled apart and her heart split wide open.

She was defenseless against him. She'd never experienced anything as fearful and thrilling all at once—as if the solid earth had fallen away beneath her feet and she was falling down a mile-high cliff with nothing to save her from a hard and lethal fall.

Nothing, except Brody.

"I'd like to head back with you." His rumbling baritone wrapped around her like the comfort of a warm electric blanket.

"You would?" *Wow, that was brilliant conversation, Michelle. Impress him, why don't you?*

He didn't seem to be paying attention to her lame words. He was staring at her. Did she dare to hope that was tenderness she saw in him?

No, she didn't believe it. If he loved her, wouldn't he have said something about it by now?

She turned away, moving on autopilot, inserting her foot in the stirrup. She hopped up into the saddle, pulled her leg over and settled into the seat.

Why was she on autopilot? Because she was watching Brody. He rose into the saddle like a pro. He was masculine grace and quiet control as he held the leather reins in his left hand, loose and low, just over the saddle horn.

Like a true horseman, he balanced easily between the stirrups, his weight shifting effortlessly as he placed pressure with his heels and Jewel eased forward.

What a man. Her entire being sang with the praise.

What was she going to do now? She loved Brody. More with every passing second. How was she going to hold back her heart?

Without an answer and with no defense, Michelle kept Keno a few paces behind Jewel.

Brody made his horse fall back and into place beside her.

Great. Now she had to talk to him. The longing within her was so powerful, it hurt like a gash from a sharp blade.

"What is a pretty lady like you doing unescorted on a Sunday afternoon?" His deep voice resonated along her skin like the wind, like the sun.

She wished he didn't affect her that way.

"I was out riding with Jenna."

"You do that a lot?"

"Since we were both in first grade."

"Practically lifetime friends. That must be something, to have a friendship like that. To have a life like that."

"I'm grateful." She knew that was a lame response but it was all she could think of to say. Nothing else came to mind.

What was she going to talk to him about? About how she was falling for him? *Thank you very much, but no!*

Brody cleared his throat. "Does she live very close?"

"The next farm on the back side of our land. We always meet at the fork at the river, halfway between our houses and ride for miles and miles. And talk."

"Women talking. There's a surprise." Brody's grin was slow and mellow.

His smile made her ache all the way down to her soul.

Why his smile? Why this man? Feeling this way was torture. To know that he didn't love her in return. He was unaware how much he was hurting her, but he was doing it all the same.

"You think all I do is talk on the phone and shop, right?" She braced against his answer, already knowing what he was going to say.

"That was my first impression of you."

There, she *knew* it. Was this the place where he broke her heart? Told her with a gentle hint that he wasn't interested? She braced herself for the worst.

"Then I took a closer look at the pretty girl who rescued me, and guess what I saw?"

His warmth had her looking up. Had her noticing there was no derision on his face, no disdain the way it had been on Rick's, the only other man she'd let this close. No. What she saw was something as rare and as tender as the love in her heart.

"I saw one of the most lovely women I've ever met." He gruffly cleared his voice and Jewel sped up the pace.

Michelle urged Keno forward. "*What* did you say?"

"I said it's a sorry state when circumstances force a man like me to be rescued by a woman like you. I thought you were an angel, you know. With all your golden hair. The way it shimmers like platinum in the sun."

Was he serious? Michelle's jaw dropped. She couldn't think of a single thing to say. Tears burned in her eyes. This couldn't be real, could it? Why wasn't he letting her down gently? Why was he making her love him even more? No one, *ever,* had said such nice things to her.

"Of course, you didn't know that you were helping a renegade like me."

Oh, so *this* was how he was going to let her down. By telling her all his faults, that he wasn't good for her, and so she shouldn't want to harbor romantic feelings for him. Okay, she could see what he was doing.

She could handle it. She was ready. Why wait? Her heart was already breaking. "You're a renegade, huh? I suppose you're going to say next that I shouldn't get mixed up with a bad guy like you. Is that it?"

He winced, as if he were in pain. As if she'd hit

the mark. He cleared his throat, but his voice remained gruff and gravely. "You're right. I shouldn't be here with you. You shouldn't trust me."

"Why? You've made no promises. You've had no reason to lie. You work hard. Dad *compliments* you. I actually heard him."

"Well, so, I painted his garage. I fixed his tractor when it broke down in the field. I know how to hay."

"Do you know how rare Dad's compliments are? They are like the Olympics. It only comes around once every four years. Well, until they started doing it every two, but still."

She charmed him. Brody hid his chuckle because he didn't want her to think he was laughing at her. Her beautiful and buoyant spirit drew him like the moon to the earth, and she pulled at the tides within him.

He ought to be resisting her. Keeping this strictly professional. And what did he want to do? Hold her hand. Kiss her. Tell her how he truly felt. It was wrong, but he couldn't help it. He couldn't stop how he was feeling. It was like trying to stop the earth from revolving around the sun.

His love for Michelle was tugging at him, tearing at his resistance. Making him wish for a future.

Maybe he didn't have to choose. Maybe he could love her and do his job. He was a good agent. He was a strong-willed man. He could separate the personal feelings from the professional.

It hadn't escaped him that Friday night she'd

planned an evening with her sister. Or last night, Saturday night, another big date night, she'd spent talking with girlfriends over ice cream and hot chocolate in the back booth of the town's diner—Hunter had noticed when he'd been tailing Mick.

Here goes nothing, he thought, and prepared for rejection. "I noticed you haven't been dating anyone. A pretty woman like you must have men knocking at your door all the time."

"I don't date random guys."

Good. Okay. That's what he would have guessed, but he had to make sure. "You *do* date, though, right?"

"I've been known to say yes now and then."

"I suppose you'd like to get married one day. I mean, don't all women?"

"I don't want to marry some farmer guy just to get married. I especially don't want to marry anyone who can't see me."

"What does that mean? Who couldn't see you? You're lovely and charming and amazing. All a man has to do is look." Couldn't she see that? Couldn't she see how much he loved her?

She bowed her head, and the brim of her hat hid her expression. She seemed sad. "You don't have to compliment me. I'm all grown up. I know what you're trying to say."

"You do?" That didn't bode well. He knew for a fact she liked him. What had she called it? A major crush. That was a good place to start building a relationship, right?

"I don't want to marry just anybody." She said it with certainty, and she sat tall in her saddle. Chin held high, she sent her horse into a faster walk. "I don't want some man who sees what you probably see."

That confused him. What was she getting at? She didn't want some man like him? No, that couldn't be right. "What do you mean?"

"You see a ditz with a cell phone and credit cards."

Is *that* what she thought? Hadn't she been listening? What was hurting her? He could feel her pain as if it was *his* heart that had been broken. His trust. His belief in himself. What had happened? This had something to do with the old boyfriend. That wrinkle-free, self-impressed Rick.

She whipped away and urged Keno into a full gallop. Before Brody could react, she was far ahead of him. All he could see was the back of her horse, Keno's black tail breezing out behind him as he galloped faster, poetry in motion. Michelle balanced in the saddle, her spine straight, her shoulders square, her golden hair streaming in the wind.

"Michelle!"

She didn't draw her horse to a stop. No, she sent him into an all-out run.

He pushed Jewel as fast as she could go, eating up ground, flying over the worn path through the field. Gaining distance. Focused totally on Michelle. On closing the distance between them. Her horse was fast. A good strong Arabian, but his mount was faster. He asked her for more, and the mare gave everything she had.

He was helpless. Until he reached Michelle's side, he couldn't do anything for her. She was in pain. He could feel it. Was she as afraid as he was? Afraid to risk everything for the chance at real love?

He had to tell her. He was terrified, but he was brave. He was strong. He couldn't let her hurt like this for one moment longer. He had to reach her. He had to stop her before she went through that gate and into the yard. Or he felt as if he'd be losing everything. This was his only chance.

He was almost there. She'd stopped Keno at the gate and was reaching down to unlock it from her lofty position in the saddle. He had time, he would get to her before she went through. He nosed Jewel directly toward the gate and used the horse's body to block it.

Michelle didn't look up. The brim of her hat hid her expression, but he didn't have to see her to know she was crying. He could feel her emotion in his own heart, as if she were a part of him.

How amazing was that? Before he met Michelle, he didn't believe in soul mates. He didn't believe in love at first sight. He didn't believe in true love.

Brody knew this connection he had with Michelle and the infinite love he felt for her couldn't be by chance. God had meant for this to be.

So he shouldn't be afraid. And neither should she.

He had to make this better. He had to fix her unhappiness. Show her there wasn't one thing to be afraid of because he'd die before he said one word to hurt her.

As if it were the most natural thing in the world, he cupped her lovely face with the palm of his hand. How soft she felt, like the finest silk. The glow within him strengthened, warming the cold places in his soul. His love for her was phenomenal, stronger than steel, unlike anything he'd ever known.

And he knew that's what God meant love to be.

Risking everything. His heart. His future. His soul. He simply told her the truth. "You are lovely. Like a fairy tale come true in my lonely life, and I love you."

Her eyes filled with tears. She didn't move. She didn't breathe. Brody went ice-cold. She didn't love him?

Then he saw the smile radiating across her beloved face.

And into his soul.

Chapter Eleven

Would it be another long week of not seeing Michelle? Brody hated to admit it, but not being around her was killing him. And why?

Because he'd risked everything. He'd stood out on a limb and told her how he felt. She hadn't said the words in return, and now the next step was hearing her say that she loved him. She cared about him. Was it too much to hope for more?

What about his mission? Working beside Mick wasn't helping to gain the man's trust. If anything, he was earning the counterfeiter's *distrust*. Mick had warned him twice about breaking Michelle's heart, that he wasn't going to stand for that as if he were a tough guy who could take Brody down.

All Brody needed was his thumb to put the overblown man on the ground and in handcuffs, but he didn't mention that. He merely tried to reply honestly, that he had no intention of hurting Michelle. He respected her too much.

And while his words and his hard work earned Pete's approval, Mick kept his distance. It wasn't hard to see why. Mick did as little as possible, and Pete wasn't happy with him.

''Is that what you're going to do when this is yours?'' Pete would ask. ''I don't want this land to go to ruin, Mick.''

I'll buy it from you. It was all Brody could do not to blurt out those words. He would bite his bottom lip and keep working. But he could buy the land. At least, his nest egg would go a long way toward a down payment on property like this.

Mick had wandered off with some muttered excuse and after twenty minutes passed, he was missing. Was the man just ducking out of field work? Or was he sneaking off to meet his contact?

Please, Father, help me to end this mission well. But quickly. How could he keep this up for much longer? Keeping secrets from Michelle, spying on her family, having everything he'd ever wanted so close, but he couldn't seize it.

His phone vibrated—Hunter left a text message. Mick had been spotted leaving the ranch on the back service road.

What was Mick up to? Itching for some action and eager to bring this case to a close so he could get on with his life, Brody almost walked away from the fieldwork. He felt it in his guts—this was the break they'd been waiting for.

The cutter jammed and clattered to a dead stop.

"I'm askin' the Lord to help me hold my temper, because that's the only way I'm gonna stay calm with a thunderstorm headed this way." Pete tossed his hat to the ground. "Brody, think you can help me? Where's Mick, that's what I'd like to know."

My partner could tell you, Brody thought as he crouched down on his hands and knees, eating dust and shredded bits of grass. He bellied under, careful of the dangerous blades, and took a look.

"You've got a length of wire caught up in here. Must have picked it up with the grass."

"And with a storm coming in, too." Stress hardened Pete's voice. His face wore the brunt of it. He looked worn and tired. He studied the seasonal workers he'd hired—a handful of teenagers. "I've got hay to put up before the hail hits. The rest of us can load if you'd run to town. Take my truck. I'll give John a call at the hardware store. He'll have the part waiting for you."

At least it would give Brody a chance to get away and give Hunter a call. Find out what was going on. "I'll take care of it. We'll have that part in and running after lunch."

"Son, you're a good man. Let me grab my phone so I can make that call." Pete yanked open the truck door, found his cell phone on the floor. "I sure thank the Lord for sending you my way."

"I thank Him for sending me here."

Pete nodded in approval as he waited for the phone to connect. "You stop by the diner and ask

Jodi to pack us up lunch to bring back with you. She'll put it on my tab.''

''Will do.'' Brody hopped in Pete's rig and headed straight to town.

He called Hunter first thing and found out that it looked as if Mick was heading for the closest casino. They already had sensitive mikes in place, in case Mick was doing business while he gambled.

''If you are right, Brody, if Mick's exchanging the money he's printing, we may end this case tonight, tomorrow morning at the latest.''

''The bearer bonds I found in his safe were a huge clue.'' Those midnight excursions had paid off. ''We're a good team, Hunter. Buzz me if you get anything else.''

''No problem.''

The second he put away his phone, his mind went back to Michelle.

How wrong was that? He couldn't seem to help it. This case was almost in the pan, he could feel it. He'd never wanted an assignment to end so fast. He couldn't waste another minute.

How was she going to feel when she found out why he was really here? Troubled, he didn't notice the reduced speed sign at the edge of town. He hit his brakes, but the town sheriff must have been patrolling somewhere else.

Maybe he'd drive on by the hardware store, see if Michelle was busy at the hair salon. Then he'd circle back for the part. When he spotted her car in the lot, the warm glow in his chest brightened.

He couldn't wait to see her. He'd missed her smile and her quick humor and her spirit.

There she was! A wave of excitement washed over him. He was about to undertake a new mission. The most important of his life. The quest to make Michelle his wife.

Fully aware Brody was standing outside the salon's wide front windows, Michelle kept her back turned. She focused her full attention on her newest customer. Just the right shade of a handsome dignified blonde bounced in a sassy layered cut. Michelle was happy—she'd done a great job, if she did say so herself. Fran, the clerk from the hotel that first night Brody came to town, stared unblinking in the large mirror.

"That's me? Why, I haven't looked this good since I was thirty."

"You're beautiful. Look at you."

"Honey, I feel like a whole new woman." Smiling broadly, Fran reached inside her purse. "What do I owe ya? I insist on paying. I haven't been this happy with a cut and style since I don't know how long."

"I said complimentary and I meant it, and we're not done yet." Michelle caught her co-worker's eye in the mirror. "Cassie is slow today. Why don't you let her treat you to a manicure? She includes a hand massage to die for."

"Oh, I've always wanted those French-tipped nails. Thank you, Michelle." Fran grabbed her into a hug. "You are just a doll. I feel so good, I swear I could bust."

Michelle heard the door behind her jangle as she led Fran to Cassie's table. Confident boots tapped on the other side of the partition. Michelle didn't have to look around to know who those boots belonged to.

Before he opened the door, she could sense his presence, as tangible and as certain as the breeze from the air conditioner against the back of her neck. The tiny hairs at her nape prickled and her entire being felt as if it were blossoming, like summer's first rose.

I love you. His words were inside her, and she felt so vulnerable. Afraid and thrilled and uncertain.

The love so new to her heart was deep. What was going to happen? What if he let her down, the way Rick had? Or what if Brody decided the open road and his life elsewhere had a greater hold on him than his love for her?

So many doubts crowded together in her mind.

No, don't think that way. She stopped the doubts, but the echoes of them remained. The uncertainty breaking her hopes a little. She grabbed the broom from the closet and swept up the hair clippings on the black-and-white tiled floor.

Could she stop thinking about him for even one minute? No. Even when he was in the other room, she could feel him. She wanted to turn to him. To her dream.

How could a man be so wonderful? It was as if

the angels had looked deep into her secret wishes, the ones she dared not voice, and brought her Brody.

This was how dangerous love was? Sure, love was tenderness and commitment and joy. She'd learned the hard way that it was also confusion and doubt and fear. Despite her worries, the love within her rose so strongly, like a river flooding its banks, taking over.

She *did* love him.

"I came to town to fetch a part, and your dad said to stop by and order up lunch from the diner." Brody's voice. Brody's step behind her as she swept the clippings into the dustpan and emptied it neatly into the small garbage can by the supply closet.

Would it be too forward if she ran to him and begged to know the feel of his arms holding her close? *Yes.*

"Want to come with me?"

I'd follow you anywhere, and that's the problem. She decided not to clue him in on that little bit of information. She straightened and put the broom and pan away and tried to sound sensible, as if she wasn't so in love with him she couldn't think straight. "Fran was my last appointment for the day. I don't have to start my shift at the coffee shop for a few hours."

"Then come with me. I'll buy you lunch while we wait."

"Make it a milk shake and you have a deal."

"Excellent." It was there in the way he watched her. Tender. Respectful.

Was this longing she felt for him part of his long-ing, too?

She grabbed her purse and slung the thin leather strap over her shoulder. With keys in hand she called goodbye to Cassie. Brody held the door for her and, when he fell in stride beside her on the sidewalk, wrapped her hand in his.

Like a couple. Like a man saying, "This is the woman I love and I choose to be by her side." She was proud to be seen with him, not because he was a good-looking man. But because he was the best man she'd ever met. And to think that he loved her.

She loved him with all the joy in her heart, even if she trembled inside. Love was scary. It was open-ing up a part of herself that she'd protected for a long time. She trusted that Brody, so protective and good, would never hurt her.

Trust. It was hard to hand over to a man again. But to *this* man it was right.

She'd never loved another human being the way she loved Brody. Even walking beside him, she ached in ways she couldn't explain. She only knew that she'd never felt so much. Been so alive. It was invigorating to see the world like this, the brightness, the colors and the brilliance.

And to feel the depth of her heart—and his.

How could she not? He fit perfectly into her life. Her family loved him. After the Monopoly game, her sisters and brothers-in-law couldn't say nice enough things about him. And her father had given Brody rare praise numerous times for his hard work in the fields. Her dad wasn't as young as he used to be, and it was hard for him to depend on others to do the work he loved.

Brody opened the heavy diner door, a perfect gentleman. His hand found hers again as they stepped into the cool breeze from the air conditioner and looked around. Only a few booths were occupied. This time of year was a busy one in farming country, and only the old-timers were talking over food and coffee today.

The waitress circled around the counter with a pot of steaming coffee in hand. "Hi, Michelle, and is this the handsome Brody I've been hearing about? What can I get you two?"

"I'd like an order to go," Brody said. "Can I see a menu?"

"I've been doing to-go's all day. Here, take this, find a booth and just wave me down when you're ready. Would you like some coffee while you wait?"

"Something cool sure would be good. Got some iced tea?"

Michelle chose a booth in the corner right beneath the air conditioner vent and slid onto the cool padded seat. "You look beat. Dad's been working you hard."

"Yep, but I don't mind. It's honest work, and I admire your dad a lot. He's a good man." Brody settled across the table from her. He looked uncertain before he reached out and drew her hand into his. "I've missed you."

His hand was iron-strong, but he trembled, a tiny bit. Or maybe she was the one who was trembling. "I've missed seeing you, too."

His fingers squeezed hers more tightly, as if holding on. As if he never wanted to let go. "Did I tell you how beautiful you look today?"

"Not yet. I'm waiting." She liked making him chuckle. He had a nice laugh—warm and deep and quiet.

"You do. But what about me? I'm covered with grass and dirt and grease. I'm surprised you aren't ashamed to be seen with me." Brody felt ashamed now that he realized he'd been so eager to see her he hadn't given a single thought to how he must look after being in the fields since four o'clock.

"I like the way the way you look." Her big eyes filled with admiration.

His throat closed up tight with emotion. She might not have said that she loved him, but the way she was looking up at him said it all.

He couldn't find the words, but he was grateful. He held her hand more tightly, wondering about her slender fingers. He had a hold of her left hand, and he figured that was no coincidence. How right his ring would feel on her fourth finger.

He felt a strange flutter as his stomach tumbled, but he was determined. He'd ask her tonight. He would find out one way or the other if she loved him. If he had a chance of making her his wife.

"If it storms, I won't be working." Did he really

sound that awkward? He cleared his throat and tried again. ''I was wondering if you'd like to spend some time with me—''

A shadow fell across the table, and it wasn't the waitress's. Michelle tried to pull her hand away, but he didn't let go. Even when the slick dressed man stared disdainfully at their locked hands.

''Oh, hi, Rick.'' Michelle didn't sound happy to see him.

Brody felt his defenses rise.

''Michelle.'' He nodded, his baseball cap shading his face. ''Hear you have a new boyfriend. A biker boyfriend.''

Brody took in the man's mocking tone and the tilt of derision of his upper lip. It took only a second for Brody to see Michelle's distressed look of pain.

He nearly leaped to his feet, overwhelmed with determination to protect her. Fierce with it. ''Good to meet you, now move on.''

''Fine. Here's a hint. Her father won't give you the land, and she's locked at the knees. Good luck.''

Brody saw red. It all happened so fast. He heard Michelle's gasp of pain, and he was on his feet. His hands full of collar and quaking with fury.

''Apologize to the lady,'' he growled.

''S-sorry,'' Rick gurgled, and Brody released him.

''Now go.'' Adrenaline pounding as hard as his fury, Brody stood protectively beside Michelle. It wasn't a peaceful response and it wasn't right, but his fury came from an honest place. From the need to shelter her. To keep her safe.

Rick straightened his cotton shirt, looked as if he were thinking over his options and then swaggered to the door.

Brody trembled, all fight, ready to keep defending her until the door closed tight.

The waitress bounded down the aisle with an iced tea and a strawberry milk shake. "Goodness, Michelle, are you all right? He didn't make you cry?"

He stepped aside, keeping his gaze on Rick through the long wall of front windows. Letting Rick know Michelle was his now. The woman he loved. He wasn't going to let anyone hurt her. Ever. On his life. On his honor.

"I'm fine, Jodi." Michelle's voice was wobbly, and her eyes were bright, but she wasn't crying.

Good thing, because Brody didn't think he could take seeing her cry.

"Some men have it all wrong. They think money is what's important, when it's the love of a good woman," the waitress soothed.

"Thanks, Jodi."

Brody heard Michelle's single sniff and she cleared the emotion from her voice. Rick had crossed the street and climbed into a brand-new sports car, red and polished and sleek. Brody might drive a sensible sedan and his town house back home in Virginia was modest, but it wasn't the net worth that made a man, but how he lived and how he treated his woman.

When Brody sat back down, his anger was fading and he realized the waitress was gone and Michelle was stirring the long handled spoon in her thick pink shake. She looked unhappy. Regret kicked in his chest.

"Sorry. I acted before I thought." He was a man of faith. He didn't go around intimidating people. What was wrong with him? He was an FBI agent.

"Thanks. No one's quite stood up for me before. Not like that, anyway." It was in her eyes. Her appreciation. Her love for him. "I thought Rick was a wonderful boyfriend. He seemed wonderful because he knew what I wanted and he was careful to give me the dream of it."

"Marriage?"

"Romance, marriage, everything." She blushed and stirred the spoon around in her milk shake. "He said that he respected me for wanting to wait until I was married to, well, *you know,* but he was cheating on me with another woman."

Rage thundered through Brody's blood with enough power to blow him apart. The edges of his vision blurred. How could anyone hurt Michelle? How could anyone not want her?

"Rick did the very worst thing he could. He betrayed me. He deceived me. He was dating me because he was hoping to get his hands on my family's net worth. He used me. He lied to me. He knocked my feet out from under me for a while."

He leaned across the table and cupped her face in the curve of his palm. Wiped a single tear from her cheek with the pad of his thumb. "Beautiful, he is the dumbest man alive to think the land was more valuable than you. You're the true value. The kind a man waits all his life to find."

She fell even more in love with him.

He pressed a kiss to her cheek, so sweet and tender it brought tears to her eyes.

This man had protected her, defended her and loved her. She couldn't find the words, so she pressed her face against his palm. She gave thanks that he felt this connection, too, the way their hearts beat in synchrony.

The way he fit against her soul.

Chapter Twelve

The thunderstorm held off. The tall stack of thunderheads amassed on the northwestern horizon as if gathering strength, waiting to attack.

Brody could feel the threat in the air. When the storm came, it would be with a fury. They worked all out, as fast as they could go. When the first gust of wind blew in cold and mean, they worked faster.

Some of the hired teenagers hurried off to help at home, to prepare for the storm. Pete and Brody kept working, fighting the wind gusts as they covered the stacked bales with tarp. The rain came and turned to hail. Lightning split the sky. They kept working.

Brody didn't mind the miserable conditions. They were good for him. He didn't think of Michelle constantly—just almost constantly. He kept picturing the love on her face as she'd pressed her cheek against his hand. Kept remembering how silken soft her skin was. How luminous her eyes were.

How he'd give anything. Do anything. Risk everything to have the right to love her. To make her his wife.

"I've got this last knot and we're done. You did good, Brody. I appreciate your hard work," Pete told him just as lightning split the sky and thunder followed within seconds. "Now you best get in while you're still in one piece, or Michelle will have my hide."

"Thanks, man."

There was nothing else to do as the hail bounced like miniature golf balls. The sound was deafening, and the pellets stung as Brody ran to his bike, strapped on his helmet, wiped his seat with the swipe of his hand and climbed aboard.

Worry troubled him as he roared down what used to be the road. It was now mud and streaming water. Hunter hadn't called. Where was he? He was feeling antsy because the sooner they could wrap up this case, the sooner he could propose to Michelle.

He splashed and slid and churned up the incline, revving the engine, both feet on the ground to give the bike enough balance and pull in the thick mud. He felt his cell phone vibrate against him—two buzzes. It was business. It was urgent. He idled the bike at the crest of the rise and dug the phone out of his pocket. "Brody here."

Static crackled in his receiver. It was Hunter's voice. "It was tough getting the warrant, but we did it. We've got Mick's middlemen on tape and we've ID'd them. I'll send you the electronic file."

"Great." That meant the end was in sight.

There was static and then Hunter continued. "We're moving in a team. Be ready to—"

Lightning ripped through the sky overhead. Thunder crashed with such fury the ground quaked beneath Brody's boots.

"Hunter?" The line was dead. After a few more tries, he gave up and jammed the phone into his pocket.

How soon would they move in? How long did he have? He had to get to a landline and see if—

A white fork of lightning jabbed from the sky to the earth, about an eighth of a mile from where he was. Deafened by the thunder, he watched sparks explode from a utility pole. Must have hit a transformer. That meant there was no power. Or phone. When he needed them most.

He sped into the wind, fighting the mud and hail until the ranch house came into sight. The windows were dark. Lightning flashed and thunder roared as night descended, stealing the last of the shadows.

There was a bob of light in the darkness ahead. A flashlight? he wondered. It was Michelle. Was she in trouble? His motor stalled, and he let it die.

He spotted her slim silhouette in the paddock. Now that he was close he could see that she was tacking a lantern to the side of the stable. The sharp terrified squeal of a panicked horse sounded like a scream. The hair raised on the back of Brody's neck.

"You need some help, beautiful?"

"If you care to lend a hand," she yelled to be

heard above the storm. She waved a lasso at the panicked mare, the large coil bunched in her hand. "How good are you at herding horses?"

"At least as good as you are."

"Then come help me, cowboy."

How could he say no to that? It was Jewel who raced by, a dark flicker of motion and substance before she disappeared into the darkness. Lightning strobed overhead with the whip crack of thunder, and Jewel went wild. She reared, her powerful front hooves slashing the air.

Astride Keno, Michelle rode with a steady calm. Brody had to admire her for that. Her voice was a low hum that did not waver as the mare came down fighting, teeth flashing, wild to attack whatever was frightening her.

Michelle was in the way as the mare charged. Brody hurled through the board rungs of the fence, fighting to get to Michelle. He had to help her. She was in danger.

No, she was in control, he realized. She tossed the lasso, the same instant she sidestepped her horse out of harm's way and the noose slipped neatly over the mare's head.

Just as the horse ducked away before the noose could pull tight and escaped. Brody endured the hail chilling him to his bones. Lightning flashed. The storm swelled.

"Throw me that lasso," he shouted.

She tossed it, a perfect throw. He ran forward to snatch it before the wind stole it. She was left with the rope coiled over her saddle—he could see her as she rode through the gleam of the lantern, and then there was darkness.

They didn't need to speak. He knew what she intended to do, and he moved without question toward the far end of the paddock. The mare was between them; he could see Michelle's shadowed outline moving against the utter blackness of the night.

Brody and Michelle worked together, driving the mare forward. Lightning shattered the darkness, blinding and bright. As thunder answered, the mare reared up, and its powerful hooves ripped into the air. Aiming right at Michelle.

Back! Michelle yanked on the reins, willing Keno to move before the mare's front hooves began to fall.

"Michelle!" She heard Brody's warning a nanosecond before the blow came.

Pain shot across the top of her shoulder and knifed down her arm, but Keno saved her, wisely moving as she directed. She wouldn't worry if she was hurt. She had to save her dad's horse. Jewel was going to hurt herself. She was beyond all sense.

Michelle shook out her noose and threw. The rope caught the mare neatly this time, and she was ready, pulling Keno back before Jewel could toss the noose. Michelle wound the rope around her saddle horn as Keno sat back, keeping the rope taut until Brody's lasso sailed high and into place. They brought the mare in.

Brody closed the doors behind her and fetched the lantern to light the way to Jewel's stall. No longer able to see the lightning, Jewel's panic faded to a skin-prickling terror. Michelle calmed the mare enough to cross tie her safely in her stall.

"Is she going to be all right?"

"Doesn't look like she's injured, just scared." Michelle grabbed a currycomb from the shelf in the aisle and got to work, talking calmly. "You sure worked yourself up, didn't you, girl?"

Leaving her to the mare, Brody unsaddled Keno, grabbed a jug of grain from the barrel in the feed room and let the gelding lead the way to his stall. It was clean and fresh with sweet-smelling straw—all Brody had to do was fill the trough with grain and fork in some hay.

It had been a long time since he'd cared for a horse, and it felt good. Right. He took it as a sign he was right where he belonged.

He took the comb from Michelle's cold fingers. "You sit down. I'll towel her off. I want to look at your arm."

"It's just a scratch. Look, it's already stopped bleeding."

Brody lifted one lantern to see for himself. "That should be bandaged. Come upstairs with me."

"It's more of a bruise. She got me with the outside of her hoof. How about you? You're a muddy mess."

He looked down. She was right. From the dirt from the fieldwork and the mud from the paddock, he was covered from hat to boot. "I'll shower, you go home and change and meet me at my place. I'll entertain you with dinner, candlelight and Scrabble.''

''You've said the magic words. I'll be there. The electricity is out. What are we going to do for food?''

''I'll start a fire in the fireplace and we'll roast hot dogs. Not romantic, but hey, I guess I'm a cheap date.''

How he could make her laugh. Brighten even the stormiest evening. ''It's a deal. I bet I can find the makings for s'mores in Mom's pantry.''

''Can't wait to spend time with you.'' He thumbed away a speck of mud on her chin. ''When I'm not with you, I miss you so much.''

She couldn't think, so she couldn't answer. His touch was like heaven, like the promise of peace and adventure all at once. Like being thrilled. Like coming home.

''Because I love you.'' Tough words for a tough guy to say, but he did it. ''Maybe I'll have to stay around when the haying's done. So I can be with you.''

How would she respond to that?

He'd traveled the country hunting bad guys, computer hackers, terrorists and criminals. He'd been undercover in extremists groups, criminal crime rings and nothing—ever—had frightened him like this. Terrified him down to his soul.

Standing before her with his heart on the line, no gun would protect him. No SWAT team could swoop in and save him.

Michelle, with her sweet-spirited gentle ways, had done what no one else could do.

She'd terrified him, she enlivened him. She made him complete.

"Yes." She looked as afraid as he felt, for this moment was a changing point for both of them. "I love you so very much. It would be wonderful if you could stay."

Tenderness overwhelmed him. A warm liquid sensation filled up his heart. His soul. He reached out— how could he not want a deeper connection to her? To this woman he'd been waiting for all of his life?

He wanted to marry her. He wanted to propose to her, but he had to do it right. Had to think it through. He wanted it to be a special moment for her to remember.

Her hair was like wet silk and smelled of strawberries and rain. Her face was rain-damp and warm as satin. He cupped her jaw, delicate against his callused fingers and, heart pounding with the importance of what he was about to do, leaned down and claimed her with a soft, slow kiss.

"Oh, Brody." She sighed against his lips.

"I didn't do too badly, then?"

"Passable."

"Is that all? Maybe I'd better try again."

"Maybe." Michelle, breathless, lifted her face to his.

Passable? No. More like paradise. Her fingers curled into the front of his shirt, holding on for dear life. No man had ever kissed her like that. With all his heart. With all he was. She melted into his kiss.

How could a simple brush of a man's lips feel like a caress to her soul? She didn't know how a man's kiss could be so incredibly tender.

The storm crashed overhead, rain hammered the roof and the horses shifted in their stalls, neighing as lightning struck. The lantern sputtered and went out.

All she knew was Brody's touch, Brody's kiss, the hammer of his heartbeat with hers.

He pulled away and gazed into her eyes. For the first time, in the pitch dark, she could see.

He was hers to love. She no longer had to hold back her heart. Keep this great affection secretly locked away. She eased into his arms, laid her cheek on his chest and savored the wonder of his strong arms enfolding her.

Michelle watched in amazement as Brody began shifting the tiles into place on the board. "I don't believe it!"

"Believe it. *Quartz.* Triple letter score. So let's see, that's forty-four points." Candlelight only improved the look of him—caressing his brow and high-cut cheekbones, the way her fingers ached to. "That puts me in the lead."

"Not for long."

"A challenge. I like that. Okay, beautiful, let's see what you've got."

Sure, he had to go and say that. As if she could

do anything with the letters she had. She had to think. And how hard was that? With the love of her life across the table from her, how was a girl to concentrate?

Then inspiration struck. "*Buzz*. There's a double letter score, so—"

"No!" Brody leaned forward, as if to see for himself. "You can't have it."

"I do." Triumphantly, she slipped the last of her tiles into place around his most recent word. "And that's thirty-four points. For the win."

"Way to go." He pushed away from the table, circling around in the shadows and knelt at her side.

She turned toward him, captivated by the shine of unconditional love in his eyes. This was happening. It really was. Brody was in love with her. And he was staying. She could already imagine their wedding—simple but elegant. And his gold band on her finger. She'd have a new name—Michelle Gabriel—and he would be her husband. Her family. And in time, there would be children. A little boy and a little girl to love and take care of.

Her life and her future were suddenly full. And fulfilling.

Because of this man kneeling before her. Because of his love.

"Come over here to the fire with me." His big hands were callused and rough textured but gentle as he led her to the crackling hearth. Soft orange light danced as if in celebration, and seemed to welcome them as she settled onto the floor, and he sat across from her. Never letting go of her.

"There are some things I want you to know about me." He looked noble, like a knight of old, a man of unshakable integrity. "I work hard. I'm an honest man. And I love you. Not for any other reason than because you are the most incredible woman I've ever met."

Could he be any more perfect?

"I'm not here because of your parents' land. Or because I'm in transition looking for a new place in life. I know you've been hurt, and you didn't deserve that."

"Everyone's been hurt." She drew his hand to her lips and pressed a tender kiss on the back of his first knuckle. "That's life. You don't have to do this, to tell me you're not like Rick. I already know that."

"You hardly know me."

"And that would take a lifetime."

How did he get so lucky? "You have no malice for Rick, do you?"

"No. I still believe in the goodness of people. Sometimes a person can get misguided, but in the end, I believe we're basically good."

That was what he needed to hear. Maybe then the twist of nerves in his stomach would calm down. "Do you know what you deserve?"

"Another s'more?"

"No. I'm serious, here."

"Sorry. I'll try to keep the jokes to a minimum."

"Thanks." He leaned forward and pressed his

forehead gently to hers. He felt a flash of connection, his heart to hers. He had to let her know. Try to make her understand.

"You deserve a man with an honest heart. A faithful soul. A man who will love you with everything he is, heart and soul for the rest of his life. When a man loves a woman like that, she's the only thing that matters to him. Not money, not pride, not comfort. He would die to protect her. Give everything to her." Gazing into her blue, blue eyes, he saw his future. In this life and beyond. "Know how I know this?"

"N-no."

"It's how I feel about you."

Big silver tears filled her eyes but did not fall. It was obvious his love mattered to her.

"You need to know this." He wasn't done, and she had to understand. If the warrant came down tonight and there was enough solid evidence for an indictment, then everything would happen too fast. There would be no time to pull her aside and make her understand.

"Shh." She was done talking and leaned forward to capture him in the gentlest of kisses.

Tenderness so perfect and powerful swept through him and made the fury of the storm outside seem small. He curled his fingers around the nape of her neck and held on. Breathed in the light faint floral scent of her perfume, only to kiss her again.

Marry me, he begged silently. Let me love and protect you forever.

But how could he ask? She didn't know that he was a federal agent. She didn't know who he was. He was here under false pretenses. Good ones, true, but he *was* deceiving her. He wanted to explain it to her, but he was sworn to secrecy.

Would she understand when the arrest was made? Would she forgive him for gathering the evidence that put her favorite uncle behind bars?

Of course she would. Look at her. She was good, through and through. She was compassionate enough to understand. To see that while he was doing a job, his love for her was the greatest truth.

"I love you." It was as honest as he could be tonight. "I want you to remember that. Regardless of what happens tomorrow, I love you, heart and soul."

She leaned into his arms and buried her face in his shoulder. She gave a little satisfied sigh. Love overwhelmed him. A deep abiding affection that was as infinite as the sky and as true as heaven.

"I love you the same way." She pressed her lips to the hollow of his throat in a quick kiss. "I'm so glad you crashed in front of me that day. What would I do if I'd never met you? I never would have known you."

Grateful to God for leading her here, for giving her this man who was perfect in every way, Michelle was too overwhelmed to continue speaking. Peace settled around them like the fire's glow.

She breathed in the masculine spicy scent of his skin and the fresh laundry scent of his shirt. She held him, just held him. This wonderful man who'd fallen into her life. A man like no other.

Her own honest, protective, faithful man.

It was fifteen minutes after one, according to his watch, and he couldn't sleep. The electricity was still off. The phone lines remained down. His cell was dead. There was no way to contact his partner or his captain.

He was worried about ending this job neatly, with no casualties. He was worried about Michelle.

The apartment held the memory of her laughter. The faint vanilla scent of the thick chunky candles she'd brought to light their way. The Scrabble game was boxed up on the table. The evening had been pleasant and companionable and complete.

He never wanted it to end.

He didn't want tomorrow to come. But the night was ticking away and soon it would be dawn. The morning raid was going to happen. Michelle was going to find out he had deceived her. There was nothing he could do to stop it.

He could only believe in the power of their love. In the goodness of her forgiving heart.

After the raid, when Mick was in custody and Michelle knew the truth, would she understand? Or would he lose her love forever?

All he could do was pray for the strength to handle what was to come.

Chapter Thirteen

"Are you up doing chores?" Michelle asked into her cell phone as she wielded her pitchfork in the dawn's first light.

"*Hello?* Where else would I be?" Jenna sounded about as thrilled as Michelle felt. "Do you have power yet? We don't. No lights, no phones."

"Bummer." Michelle gave a quick thanks that their lights had come on sometime in the night and that their cell phones were working. "No power means no electricity for the water pump. Are you packing water?"

"Oh, just a few dozen ten gallon buckets. My arms are stretched like a Gumby doll's. Really. Where's a generator when you need one? Or a big strong handsome hunk living over my garage to help me out?"

What news she had to tell Jenna. But not on the phone. With her luck, Brody would come walking down the stable aisle and overhear. Or one of her sisters would show up. Or her mom. Then everyone would know.

Besides, it felt too personal to talk about on the phone. She felt as if Brody's love was too good to be true, and if she dared to say out loud, ''I found the one. The man I want to love the rest of my life,'' then he'd vanish. Or some disaster would naturally follow.

Disaster did have a tendency to follow her around, and so she saved the news for later. ''So, do you want to go on a ride this afternoon?''

''I've got work, but I could ride by after supper and we can take the horses to Bible study?''

''Cool. Great idea!'' That would give them all the time in the world to talk. Plus, they hadn't gone on that long of a ride in ages. ''Call me.''

''Later!'' Jenna's connection went dead.

Michelle pocketed her phone and laughed when Keno gave a gentle yank on her ponytail. ''Hey, what do you think you're doing?''

The big dark brown gelding nibbled on the back of her neck, an affectionate gesture, and she put down her pitchfork to pull him into a hug. She rubbed her fingertips along his warm silken jawline and cheeks and up under his mane. He leaned into her touch, closing his eyes, wuffling softly, a low contented sound that said it all.

Yep, it was going to be a great day. The world felt at peace after the storm. The dawn's golden light was like a gentle promise of good things to come.

Larks greeted the new day. The wind was lazy, stirring against her skin.

And she was spending the morning with her very best friend, Keno. Soon, she'd ride him out to the fields to bring her dad a pot of coffee, just because. And then she'd see *him*. Brody.

The thought of him was all it took to make her feel as if she were floating. She couldn't believe it. He loved her. Not just a warm glow kind of a love, but the real thing. All the way to his soul, with he-would-die-for-her devotion.

What had he said? *I love you, heart and soul.*

The way she loved him.

Thank you, Father, she remembered to pray as she gave Keno one last rub under his chin.

She had a good life. It wasn't the excitement of a big city and it wasn't the thrill of an ambitious life, but it was all she'd ever wanted.

To wake up before dawn and watch the sun peer over the jagged edges of the breathless Bridger Mountains. To witness the day coming new to the world as she worked in the paddocks. To be with her best friends, the horses and to have her family close.

To feel the changes in the land—the planting seasons, the growing seasons, the harvest. To live where she had so many roots. This place was her entire world. She had everything her heart had ever desired.

But would she leave it for Brody? What if he asked her to?

What if he wanted to marry her, but he didn't want to live in a small town on a farm and while away the hours on the front porch?

What if his dreams were different from hers? What if he could never be happy here?

Put it in God's hands. That's what Pastor Bill always said. So, that's what she'd do. She would pray and ask the Lord to guide her. To trust that He would work these questions out in His way and in His time.

Hadn't He brought Brody to her? Surely He hadn't done that without knowing it would work out. Right?

This was no different.

She poured grain in Keno's trough and latched his stall gate. When she was putting up the pitchfork she heard it; a different sound than she'd heard on any other morning.

She rushed to the main stable doors and skidded to a stop at the sight of three sleek black SUVs, with dark-tinted windows speeding toward her uncle Mick's bungalow.

Ten minutes after five, and they were moving in, ready to make the arrest. The SWAT team was in place, situated around the perimeter of the yard, ready to protect, if necessary, the agents climbing out of the vehicles.

It was a simple plan, to keep downwind from the house with the team members in the back to make sure Mick didn't run. The hope was to arrest him unsuspecting in his truck on the road, where he was less likely to be armed and there would be less chance of a shoot-out. Where there were no passersby by to step in the line of fire.

Brody hoped to take Mick quietly, without harm to anyone.

Not to *anyone,* Brody amended, thinking of Michelle as he remained crouched in the shadows of the draw with the creek behind him, his boots in mud. He was hyped, tense with anticipation. His every sense was alert to the unexpected.

He waited soundlessly, his rifle cradled in the crook of his arm. He was ready. Prepared for the worst. Praying for the best.

"Glad this is your last mission, buddy?" Hunter broke the silence.

"You know it." This mission had been the worst, eating at his conscience. He'd lied to good people, been someone he wasn't. That was wearing on a man of faith.

How was Michelle going to take this? It troubled him. Worry burrowed deep in his stomach and didn't let up. They'd had a good evening together.

Last night, basking in the happy glow of their evening together, he'd had hope.

But this morning, in the cool damp, he was filled with trepidation. Maybe it was because of the bitter tang of adrenaline in his mouth or the tension balled in his guts. For whatever reason, he'd misplaced that hope. Lost it on the way from being Brody—the man Michelle McKaslin loved—to becoming Gabe Brody, FBI agent, armed and dangerous.

"He's coming down the stairs," crackled in his ear. It was Dan Thomas from the SWAT team. "Our target is in the kitchen. Getting his keys. Okay, this is it."

Brody felt the familiar calm spill through his veins. They were good to go. Anything could happen, and he had to be sharp, focused and prepared. He forced every last thought of Michelle from his mind and concentrated.

He realized this was the last time he'd be in danger like this. The last time he would lay his life on the line for his country. He prayed for a peaceful end. He didn't want anyone getting hurt.

And while he was at it, he would pray for God to fill Michelle's heart with understanding.

The crackle over the earpiece was the first indication something was wrong. It wasn't Dan. It was Pierce. "We've got a civilian. A woman on horseback."

"Michelle!" He was on his feet before he remembered to stay down. He only knew he had to protect her. If she got in the way and bullets starting flying, she'd be caught in the cross fire. He growled into his com, "Pierce, get her outta here."

Dan again. "He's on the move. In his truck. Team one, move in."

Brody moved fast and low. Had Pierce gotten Michelle to safety? What if she was scared? What if she tried to warn Mick?

Thoughts of everything that could go wrong and

things that had gone wrong on other missions flashed through his mind.

Pierce can handle it, he had to remind himself. He calmed his icy, near-the-edge adrenaline. He was intensely protective when it came to the woman he loved.

Concentrate, Brody. Mick's rusted old truck was bouncing down the mud-puddled lane, coming closer. The window was rolled down broadcasting classic country music. Johnny Cash crooned as two vans tore out of the underbrush and skidded to a stop in the road in front of Mick. One more from behind.

Through the cracked windshield and the scope of his rifle, Brody read Mick's confusion. *C'mon, Mick, stop. Do the right thing. Make this a peaceful arrest.*

As if Mick heard him, the truck skidded to a stop, sliding in the mud toward the creek, where cottonwoods and the deep water blocked him on one side. The cut of the hill penned him in on the other. He was trapped.

"This is the FBI. Hands up, Mick, where I can see them." Brody used the bed of the truck as a shield as he moved. Kept his weapon steady, site true and his finger on the trigger as Hunter threw open the truck's door.

"Brody?" Mick looked confused. "Is that you? What in blazes is going on here? I thought we were haying this morning."

"I'm not your friend, Mick. Now keep your hands up. Slide out nice and slow."

"Hey, I've got no beef with you. What is this

about?'' Mick took one look at all the weapons pointed at him, the very determined men in flak jackets and, holding up his hands, climbed out of the truck.

Two agents helped him to the ground.

Brody stood, feet apart, gun aimed at the back of Mick's head as the handcuffs snapped shut.

Around him men were shouting orders. The teams were moving in, the unit peeling off to search Mick's house. His safe, his computer, all his personal records would be confiscated and everything inside the house turned upside down.

It's over. The mission was done. The enormity of it sank in, and Brody removed his weapon once Mick was secure. He was free now. He'd leave Hunter in charge and find Michelle—

Wait. She'd found him. He felt her presence as surely as the sun on his back and the earth beneath his boots. A tingle of apprehension settled in his midsection. Something was wrong. *Very* wrong.

Michelle. She'd dashed onto the road, up from where Pierce had to have taken her near the creek. She stood in the muddy center of the lane, looking as fresh as the morning, as genuine as the countryside spread out around her.

She wore a pair of faded jeans and simple white T-shirt. Beneath the brim of her baseball cap, her eyes shone with tears. Her beautiful rosebud mouth, the one that had said, ''I love you,'' to him looked as if she'd tasted poison.

That poison was him.

She scanned the huge FBI letters on his chest, then his gun that had been aimed at her uncle. Her lower lip trembled and she turned away.

She didn't need to say a word. Her silence was worse than if she'd started yelling at him, calling him every name he deserved.

She ran. Ran from him as if he was the worst thing that had ever happened to her.

Ran so he couldn't see her tears.

But he could feel her heart break. Because her heart was his, too.

She knew he was behind her, so she didn't bother to look over her shoulder to see it for a fact. She could feel him, sense him. And why? Because he was the love of her life. The man God meant especially for her.

It wasn't a surprise that she could feel the man who was meant to be a part of her forever, was it? No. And that made her even more mad. Made her hurt more.

Brody. He'd *lied* to her. He'd *used* her. She'd seen his jacket. His rifle. *FBI* had been blazed across his chest and his back.

"Michelle!"

She did not want to talk to him. After what he'd put her through! First, she'd been scared when she saw the black vans speeding toward her uncle Mick's house. It wouldn't be the first time old friends or people who'd loaned money to him showed up a little angry.

But when a gunman crept out of the brush by the creek and asked her to keep down for her own safety, and to come with him—

"Michelle! Wait up. I need to talk to you."

I don't care what you need. What *she* needed was a good hard stick to smack him upside the head with.

Well, not that she could actually hit anyone, but the thought of it made her feel better. Anger turned her bright red inside, and beneath that was the crumbling sensation of her being wrenched into pieces. It felt as if every part of her, heart and soul, was broken and bleeding.

"Michelle." His hand lighted on her shoulder, a silent offer of comfort.

And that was the problem. She didn't want his comfort. She wanted to hate him. She just wanted this pain inside her to leave, so she could curl up somewhere all by herself and cry until there were no more tears.

He'd deceived her. Pretended to love her. How could he do such a thing? And she'd thought he was perfect.

Too upset to speak, she did manage to shove his hand away. She walked fast, even though her vision was blurry. There were *not* tears in her eyes. Okay, there were. But they were *angry* tears. She was angry, not hurt. Furious, not betrayed. Outraged, not shattered.

"I'm sorry."

"I bet you are." She whipped through the grass, faster.

He stayed on her tail. "I was under oath. I couldn't tell you."

"I understand." Oh, she understood. She'd been the biggest fool of all, falling for his line. Another man telling her what she wanted to hear for his own purposes.

How dense was she? "For your information, I'm not some romantic sap of a fool. I see what you wanted. You needed to get on the property to arrest Mick and you tricked me."

"No, I never tricked you." He loped alongside her in his black jacket and gear. The white letters across his chest proclaiming his identity for the entire world to see. The FBI?

He'd used her. So he could arrest her uncle.

Keno looked up from grazing, nickered a welcome low in his throat. She yanked his reins from the low cottonwood she'd tied him to and knocked into Brody's arm as she turned.

"Out of my way."

"No. I want you to listen to me." He grabbed her with both hands, holding her so tight, with what felt like so much need.

Oh, he was good. Very good at playing his role. Oh, yeah, she saw it all in a flash. The big white *FBI* on his chest said more than he ever could.

Whatever Mick had done, he'd done it big this time, and that's why Brody was here. That's why Brody had wormed his way into her family and into her heart. That's why he seemed so perfect, because he'd planned it all along.

And she, like the biggest fool ever, invited him right in.

"I can explain this, Michelle. Give me the chance. Please."

"What could you possibly have to say to me?"

"Everything. Let me explain."

"I think your gun says it all." He looked like some stealthy warrior, all dressed in black, with his semiautomatic weapon slung over his left shoulder on a strap. He was all steel as he held her, his grip an unbreakable band on her upper arms. "Let go."

"No, I can't. I told you the truth, everything but—"

"Let go of me."

It was the cool sound in her voice, the icy pain that shocked him enough to let go. Brody took a step back. His heart broke with her pain.

She was going to leave him. She wasn't going to understand. She wasn't going to give him a chance. And he'd hurt her. He'd gone back on his word and he'd made her cry.

He had to fix this. He had to stop those tears. Make her stop hurting. "Michelle, what I said last night. That was the truth. I said regardless of what happened today, I love you. Do you remember that?"

She made a "huh!" sound and straightened the stirrup, fit her foot into it and rose up into the saddle.

This wasn't working. What should he say? He could see the sheen of tears on her face. See the pride in the straight set of her back.

He caught hold of her ankle. He had to get through to her. Had to make her see. "I love you, and that was as true yesterday as it is today. As it will be tomorrow."

"You deceived me." She swiped at the tears on her cheeks with the back of her hand. Her eyes shimmered but more didn't fall.

He could feel her disillusionment. She was like a steel wall set against him.

He would give anything to take that wall down. To turn back the clock to last night, when he'd had the privilege of holding her close. "I never lied about the way I feel for you. That's the truth, Michelle."

"You're not a rodeo rider. You weren't traveling on your bike to sightsee. You never grew up on a farm, did you?"

"That was the truth. The farms, my dreams, how I feel about you. That's me. You know what's real about me. From the moment I first saw you, I was captivated. I never hid who I really am from you."

"You're an FBI agent. You hid that pretty well."

"You have every right to be mad, but please, let me fix this. I can't bear to know I'm making you cry."

"Oh, you're not. I'm crying because I'm mad at myself. I put my faith in you, and I shouldn't have. Shame on you."

She looked at him as if he were a stranger. A detestable stranger.

She was right. He didn't feel fit to stand on the

ground in front of her. He wasn't good enough to breathe the same air.

Brody had never felt such shame. Agony squeezed so tight in his chest, he couldn't breathe as she turned her horse toward home.

"Can you forgive me?"

She turned in the saddle. "I understand. You were simply doing your job."

"No. I fell in love with you."

"Stop saying that." He was tearing her apart, and for what? So he could walk away from this with a clear conscience?

Didn't he understand that she still loved him? How wrong was that? He'd made her believe she was exciting enough and wonderful enough that a man like him could love her forever.

When all along he'd—

No, she couldn't think it, or she'd fall apart and there was no way she was about to let him know what he'd really meant to her. If nothing else, she was going to keep what she had left of her dignity.

Lord, help me find wisdom. She had to pull it together. She had to let him know she was just fine.

Dying inside, she firmed her spine, lifted her chin and looked at the man who'd used her and betrayed her. It was easy to see that he *was* sorry for it.

Sorry he'd made her believe something that could never be true. No matter how much it hurt, she held back her last tears. "Good luck to you in the future."

"Is there a chance—?" He looked like she felt—raw and bleeding.

Brody. Her heart cried out for him. Her love was so fierce for him, it tore her to pieces. She wanted him to be different. To go back to last night when he was her one true love.

How could she?

Her soul ached, empty, as she turned away. What else could she do? She urged Keno into a gallop as fast as his strong legs could carry them.

When Brody was just a lone figure on the distant field, she drew her horse to a stop. Slid from the saddle. Knelt in the grass. Let the tears come. Hot, wrenching, consuming.

She felt the soft velvet of her horse's nose against her jaw, nuzzling at her tears. Her best friend. Her trusty gelding she'd loved for most of her life. He loved her no matter what.

"Some males are pretty darn faithful and true." She leaned her forehead against his neck, grateful for his comfort. His friendship.

Not even his comfort could stop the horrible rending of her heart, of her soul.

Nothing ever would.

Michelle was on her knees and she was crying. Brody *had* to go to her. He'd vowed never to hurt her and look at what he'd done to her. To the woman he loved more than anything.

"C'mon, man, we gotta go." Hunter gestured toward the vans loading up. "Another mission done. It's your last."

Brody rubbed his hands over his face. This had gone terribly wrong. There she was, standing up. She was so far away, she was only a slim figure against the endless green.

If he went to her, would it make any difference? How could he change her mind? Repair the damage?

Hunter didn't relent. "C'mon, buddy. It's over. You've done your job and it's time to go. They're waiting."

How was he going to walk away from everything that mattered? Go home as if his time here hadn't meant everything.

"I can't believe this ended so fast," Hunter said. "Remember the Olympic Hills job? We lived in the mud and woods for a week."

"One miserable week. It rains every day of April in Portland."

Hunter chuckled. "I already knew that. Hey, this case was a piece of cake. It was a good one to ride out on. What's next for you? The wide-open road?"

That used to appeal to him. To just take off, vacation. He'd never been good at vacationing. He was always too focused on work.

That wasn't his problem anymore. His time was his own. What did he want to do with it? He only knew one thing for sure. He wanted to be here. On this piece of land. With Michelle as his wife.

She hated him. She thought he betrayed her. How

did he fix that? Surely the Lord didn't mean for things to end this way? Did He?

Hunter gazed in Michelle's direction. ''Don't tell me you've finally found the right woman?''

''That, my friend, is in God's hands. And hers.''

There she was, climbing back on her horse. She rode into the bright rays of the rising sun, golden and pure, and disappeared.

Leaving him alone. He'd lost everything.

Two agents were at the kitchen table, accepting Alice McKaslin's steaming fresh coffee with fervent gratitude as Michelle burst through the back door.

''Honey, there you are.'' Her mom looked relieved. ''I was worried. These men have questions about Uncle Mick. They need us to talk to him. He's got himself in some trouble now.''

''I need to change.'' She wanted to shower and find fresh clothes, but what she needed most was time.

Time to gather up the pieces of her shattered heart. Find a place inside her to lock them quietly away. To pull herself together.

Then she could come back downstairs and face Brody's colleagues. Oh, how they probably got a good chuckle at the country girl who fell hopelessly in love with the worldly, mysterious Brody.

Michelle kept walking and headed for the stairs.

One of the agents was talking. ''Gabe is on his way.''

''Gabe?'' Her mom asked.

"Gabe Brody," the agent clarified. "You don't know what your cooperation has meant. We want you to know your family has been cleared of all suspicion. We feared your farm and your one daughter's coffee shop were fronts for laundering counterfeit money."

"I just can't believe it. Mick! After all we've done for him. He was tossed out by his wife last year, you know. And I can see why! Counterfeiting. How could he think to do such a thing. And we couldn't bend over fast or far enough to help him."

Michelle hurried through the living room. Gabe. That was his name. Agent Gabe Brody with the FBI.

Of course he was a noble, distinguished, hardworking man. A hero that helped to keep the laws of their nation. She'd known all along he was someone special. More than a drifter on a bike in black leather.

"Everyone should have a supportive family like yours. Too bad Mick didn't make better choices with his life." The agent's words changed to a mumble as she started up the stairs.

She blinked hard. She was crying for Uncle Mick, that was all. Uncle Mick and his bad choices. Following the wrong paths. Making counterfeit money. Putting them all under the scrutiny of the FBI. Putting Brody right in the middle of their lives so he could use her for information.

Michelle stopped on the landing. There were the family pictures, all marching up neatly in carefully organized rows. Sadness wrapped around her. She'd hoped to add to the picture gallery, as Karen and Kirby had. She'd wanted that so much that it hurt.

She'd already envisioned her wedding pictures and her baby portraits. They would be framed in gold and hung at the top of the stairs, along with the others. A color documentary of the McKaslins' lives. A testimony to the abundant love they were blessed with.

Would that kind of love ever happen to her again? Brody had been pretending, but she hadn't.

Or was he her one true love, and there would never be another?

There she went, being romantic again. How foolish was that? Brody may have seemed like her true companion in this life. But it had all been an act on his part.

Maybe it wasn't.

Where did that thought come from? It was her heart still wishing for Brody. He *had* come to her afterward. He'd tried to explain. He'd said he was sorry. He'd said he still loved her.

And what if that was just an act, too?

What if it wasn't?

And if it wasn't, how did she open her heart, even crack the door, just to let in more pain?

There he was. She could see him climbing out of one of the black vans. He looked like a dream— better than a dream—dressed all in black, with his protective vest and his weapons.

He looked like a hero on the silver screen, and

she had to close her eyes. Turn away from the man who'd blown her last dream apart.

He was no strong, protective, honest man.

She was done with Agent Gabe Brody.

"She won't see you, man." Hunter came through the door of the McKaslins' garage apartment and looked around. "Nice. This was a lot better than the trailer we were stuck in, remember that job in Tacoma?"

"Or the studio apartment in east L.A.?"

"Yeah. Good times." Hunter rolled his eyes. "Well, this is it. The captain says you might as well ride out the way you came in. You've got the surveillance equipment packed up?"

Brody pointed it out stacked behind the couch, ready to go.

It was hard to watch Hunter leave. They'd worked together for ten long years. It was tough watching from the window as the agents climbed in and drove away.

That was his life, and he'd been good at it. One of the best. But it hadn't made him happy. It was the life of a loner, the life of an observer. He'd always been traveling, always been working. Being the hand of justice when necessary wasn't an easy thing.

He'd done his time, and it was over.

He'd trusted the Lord to show him what was next. To point him in the right direction.

And the Lord had.

He'd been all over the world in his work, and no place had affected him like this. No place whispered to him as if he belonged here, as if he'd been waiting for this all his adult life. And for the woman who lived in that house. Who owned his loner's heart.

Alice stepped onto the porch, squinted up at the apartment, frowned at him in the window and went back inside.

Yep, they were angry. It was a hard thing, knowing he'd duped them. He'd arrested their beloved relative. Despite his flaws, the McKaslins did love Mick.

He didn't have to be told he wasn't welcome. He left his business card on the table, in case they had questions, the office would know where to find him for a while.

It was hard to leave. Memories tugged at him. He'd told Michelle how much he loved her right here in front of the hearth. And she'd said the same.

How much did she mean it? Was she the woman he thought she was, that when she loved it was with everything she had? Heart and soul, the same way he loved her?

Only time would tell.

He grabbed his duffel, climbed down the stairs in the blistering sun and stowed his pack on the bike. No one came out to wish him well or offer their goodbyes as he started the engine.

That was just as well. He wouldn't know what to say to them.

He took one last look at paradise before he released the clutch and drove away from everything that really mattered to him. The only home he wanted to have.

The only woman he would ever love.

turned her about and Charlie's she look everything
that early morning of firmee had held it Kirby
sizzled it around
A. the pack because your becomes

Chapter Fourteen

"**O**h, I don't believe it. Tell me I counted wrong!" Michelle moaned as she dropped her little silver shoe on the hotel bearing Boardwalk.

"Looks right to me!" Kirby rubbed her hands together. "Two thousand dollars, please. If you hand over all your property and money, that should just about do it."

"I'm broke. Bankrupt." The phone rang and Michelle sprang out of the chair.

The past few weeks had been tough, but she was surviving. Tonight's game was Monopoly, because she couldn't bear to play Scrabble—her feelings were still fragile. It seemed everything reminded her of Brody. "Does anybody want anything from the kitchen?"

"Food!" Kirby called out.

"Lots of it!" Kendra seconded.

Michelle looked at the caller ID that read Federal

Government and decided to let it ring. She'd blocked Brody's number on her cell and on the house phone. She did *not* want to talk to that man. She did *not* want to get a message from that man. Now he was resorting to playing hardball. How was she going to block all the FBI offices?

The answering machine clicked on while she was pulling a new bottle of soda from the fridge. Then there was Karen, blocking her way. Karen had that look in her eye.

Michelle knew just what it was, too. After the fallout of discovering that Brody was an agent and he'd been deceiving them all, the shock had worn off and Karen and her husband were the first to be on Brody's side.

What was Karen going to do? Give her another gentle reminder that Brody had never outright lied. He had worked undercover in a rodeo. He was a good man. The face he'd shown them was authentic.

Michelle knew all that. She'd thought of nothing but Brody since she'd listened to his motorcycle rumble down their driveway, leaving her forever.

Leaving her so easily. And that's why she was certain he'd manufactured his "love" for her. Michelle doubted Karen would ever understand. How could she? Karen had the perfect life. A wonderful, trustworthy husband. A beautiful new baby. A comfortable home.

She hadn't been blown away by Brody's declarations of love. She hadn't been devastated by Brody's broken promises.

Karen headed toward the phone. "Aren't you going to answer that?"

"Nope. I'm screening calls."

"Are you sure you want to do that?" Karen stopped at the island, clearly waiting to see who was about to leave a message. "Brody called Zach last night. They struck up a friendship, you know, and Brody asked about you. He's been trying to get a hold of you. He wanted to know if you were okay."

"I'm sure." That was not a lie. She would be okay. She had to be. What she had with Brody was make-believe. What was the point in rehashing it? He'd done his job and he rode away.

Fine. Then he ought to stay out of her life. That's why she'd blocked his phone numbers and returned his letters. He was probably feeling guilty because he was a liar.

But a tiny part of her couldn't stop hoping that he wasn't. What had he said? Regardless of what happens tomorrow, I love you, heart and soul. Even now, she wanted it to be true.

How could it be? He left. If he'd loved her so much, then how could he ride away without looking back? And even if he was telling the truth about loving her, that didn't erase the fact that he'd deceived her once. Did that mean he could do it again?

She didn't know, but it ripped her in shreds to think about it.

Karen was relentless, even if she was the nicest person ever as she grabbed a new bag of potato chips from the pantry. "I like Brody. And so does Zach.

He apologized for deceiving us. He was only doing his job and he did it well. He was as respectful to our privacy as possible.''

''Oh, is that what he said.'' Making her want him didn't qualify for that, not in her book! ''He made me—''

''Love him?''

Yes. She'd tried everything she could think of to purge this unbreakable affection from her heart. The abiding love that refuse to lessen, refused to fade and remained as bright as ever. Praying hadn't stopped it. Time hadn't diminished it.

What was she going to do?

There was sympathy on her sister's face. Karen had been there to guide her and protect her like a big sister should, all of her life. ''What would you do? If Brody had been Zach, before you married him, wouldn't you have sent him packing?''

''You can never walk in another person's shoes exactly, so I don't know.'' Karen pulled out the stool at the breakfast bar and pulled the potato chip bag close so she could open it. ''I only know that in a perfect love, there is room for forgiveness. And for mistakes.''

''It wasn't a mistake. He deceived me on purpose.''

''What choice did he have?''

''True.'' Michelle hated that one point of the argument, the one she kept going over and over again no matter where she was—whether she was riding her horse, chatting with Jenna, working at the Snip

& Stylę and even when she was supposed to be studying her Bible.

The answering machine beeped and clicked. Karen had hit the play button and was turning up the volume.

It was a man's voice. "Yeah? Say, this is uh, Captain Daggers. I'm Agent Brody's supervisor and I'm trying to get in touch with Michelle McKaslin. If you could have her return my call, I would appreciate it. I want to assure her that my agent had no choice but to keep his mission from her, as it could have jeopardized innocent lives. Thank you."

As she ripped open the stubborn potato chip bag, Karen crooked one brow as if to say, *See? What else could the poor man do?*

Yeah, yeah. Michelle took her time searching for the tubs of dip. Since everyone liked something different, she had to make sure there was French onion dip or Kendra would complain. Ranch for Kirby. It was her sisterly duty. She wasn't trying to hide her tears or anything. Really. Her eyes were watering because it was cold inside the refrigerator. Really cold.

"Like I said, there is room in a perfect love for forgiveness. And mistakes."

She'd told Brody everything. She'd shown him her heart and every vulnerability. He knew what Rick had done to her and that she'd been hurt before, and still he'd lied.

She found the last tub of dip. "How can I forgive him?"

"Maybe he's not the one who made the mistake. Or needs forgiving." Karen reached across the center island to tug at Michelle's ponytail. "Think about that, baby sister."

"I didn't do anything wrong."

"Does the Bible teach us to be forgiving?"

"Well, that only goes so far. I mean, I'm not a doormat." She picked at the plastic on the tub of ranch dip. She took great care ripping off the plastic seal.

She had to take her time and do it right because she didn't want to chip her nails.

"Are you crying?"

"No."

"You love him. You really do. It's the real thing." Karen abandoned the bags of chips on the counter and wrapped her arms around Michelle. "Love like that is rare. And it hurts. It challenges us to be bigger and better people than we are. Take my advice and rise to the challenge. Show him what your heart is truly made of. It will work out, I promise it."

How did Karen know? Could she fast-forward through time to see how this was going to end?

But then, Karen did seem to know everything. She had the perfect life. She always made the perfect choices. Michelle couldn't thank God enough for the wonderful blessing of her sisters.

Brody idled the black powerful motorcycle on the shoulder of the road. The West Virginia farm country had changed since he'd been a boy, but the old red barn was still standing. Someone had put on a new roof and painted it white. It looked sharp. Sheep grazed in lush fields.

This was his past. A past he'd refused to think about because it always brought with it grief. Now there were only the happy memories. The field there, where he and his dad once rode the tractor together. And the path between the fences where he'd ridden his horse.

Good memories. He had peace, at last.

With any luck, there would be better memories to make in his future.

He'd sold his town house, had a moving company come for his belongings and now he was heading west. To Montana.

To Michelle.

Would she forgive him? She'd blocked his number, so he couldn't even ring in on her phone. She'd returned his letters. She hadn't answered his captain's call. With the way she was acting, he was probably out of luck.

But he knew she could forgive him. Why? Because he loved her. Fierce and true and forever. Nothing would ever change that love or diminish it. It was a once-in-a-lifetime kind of blessing.

He believed that was the way she loved him. And always would.

He let out his clutch and spun gravel as he pulled onto the two-lane country road that would take him on the journey home.

* * *

Not even buying shoes made her feel better. That was a sorry state to be in.

With her cell wedged carefully between her shoulder and ear, Michelle lifted her foot from the gas pedal because she'd crept up a hair over the speed limit on the two-lane country road. "I found some really great boots for when the weather cools down. Yeah, they'll look so great with jeans. I hit an end-of-season sale on sandals and got this kickin' pair of strappy flats."

"Perfect for the singles' night at church," Jenna enthused on the other end of the phone. "I wish I could have gotten off work to go with you. Maybe you'd let me borrow something? I don't have anything to wear."

"Neither do I, but come over after work. We'll get ready together."

"Cool. Later!"

"Later!" Michelle dropped her phone on the seat and blinked at the image in her rearview mirror. A black motorcycle was behind her, getting ready to pass. A man in a black T-shirt and faded denim jeans, his face hidden by his helmet.

Brody! Her heart stopped. No, it couldn't be him. This bike was a different color. It was just wishful thinking. Longing for something that could never be.

It was weird how whenever she thought of him, she ached in the place deep in her heart where she used to feel him so strongly. But the connection between them was severed. What choice did she have?

Okay, she got that he was only doing his job. But he'd captured her heart. He'd made her fall in love with him. If he'd meant it, then why did he leave so easily, as if it had all been part of the plan to gain her family's trust?

Her gaze strayed to the motorcycle lingering behind her. She flicked on her blinker and expected him to pass. But he didn't. He slowed down along with her as she turned into her driveway. He went on by. The bike had a Montana license plate.

It wasn't Brody. He was long gone. After his supervisor had called, there had been no other word from him. Sure, it made her horribly sad. The ache remained deep in her soul, where there was a constant emptiness. An emptiness that no man could ever replace.

She'd thought about what Karen said; not forgiving the one you love is a mistake. But that wasn't the only problem. That wasn't what left her unhappy even after she had new shoes on her feet.

She couldn't stop the heavy disappointment wrapped around her as she pulled into the carport. No one was around. Her mom was probably over at Gramma's. Her dad was out in the fields, cutting alfalfa. The empty house echoed around her as she ran upstairs to put her new shoes away. If she could find room for them in her closet.

What she needed to do was to force him from her mind. How? She had the rest of the afternoon. Maybe she'd take a long hard horse ride. That would do it. She'd saddle up Keno and take him on one of his favorite trails.

As she tied back her hair into a ponytail, she caught her reflection in the small dresser mirror. She was too pale and had dark circles from lack of sleep.

Jenna was right. What she needed to do was to get out. Do something new. And that's why they were going to the singles' night barbecue tonight, even though they knew every unmarried man there.

She was only going to be moral support for Jenna because Michelle was done with men. Through. Through being used. Lied to. Hurt.

She was just fine on her own. She was happy. She had friends and family. She had her horse. She had two jobs and a little too much credit card debt, but that was her own fault.

She did not need a man to be happy.

The doorbell rang.

Who could it be? It wasn't as if they were expecting guests in the middle of the day when everyone was busy on their farms.

Could it be the deliveryman? She was expecting a catalog order. Had it come already? Michelle bounded down the stairs, going as fast as she could. She couldn't wait to open the box. She'd ordered the cutest little jean jacket and it would look great on Jenna, for the dance tonight—

She flung open the door.

No deliveryman. No delivery truck. No one at all.

But there, perched on the wide rail of the front porch sat a dozen fragile pink rosebuds in a crystal

vase. Each bud was perfect, the silken edges strug-
gling to open.

On the rail, beside the vase was a wooden tray
from a Scrabble game.

From Brody.

Her legs began to tremble, and she could *feel* him.
He was nowhere in sight, but that didn't matter. He
was here. She remembered that black motorcycle behind her. That had been Brody. He must have taken
the service road instead of turning down the driveway.

He was here? She couldn't wait to see him; she
never wanted to see him again. What was she going
to do?

As if being pulling by an unseen rope, her feet
moved her forward toward the porch rail. Toward
the flowers and the nine Scrabble tiles that spelled
out Forgive Me.

She wanted to. More than anything. Was it the
right thing to do?

She could feel his presence like the hot summer
air on her skin. He was coming for her. What did
she do? How could she believe in him again? She
stared as hard as she could at the little wooden tiles.
Terror rocked her. She'd never been this afraid.
Never had so much to lose.

His boot rang on the bottom step.

Although she vowed not to, she moved toward
him. There he was, looking like a dream come true,
one boot on the bottom step, and on his knee held

with both hands was a second tray. The tiles spelled Marry Me.

Her bottom lip started to shake. No, it was impossible. He'd left so easily. He'd been playing a part. His wonderful words, his solid promises, his die-for-her love was a fabrication. Right?

"You're crying." He set the tray on the rail and moved toward her.

Could she help it? She was in his arms, letting him hold her, breathing in his comfort like air. She felt as if her heart was breaking all over again.

His hands cupped the sides of her face with great tenderness. With everlasting love. She could feel it; the places in his heart matched hers.

But how could she believe? How could she trust that this was real? That he was what he said?

"Because I love you," he answered her thoughts as if he'd heard them. The pads of his thumbs brushed away the tears on her cheeks. "I left like you wanted, and my love didn't die. It grew stronger. I told you it would."

So did my love for you. She was too overwhelmed to speak. This couldn't be real. He was a dream, her dream, and dreams ended and then a girl woke up to reality.

"My dear Michelle." He kissed her brow. "I am a man who will love you with everything I am, heart and soul, for the rest of my life."

Great silver tears filled her big eyes and spilled down her cheeks.

His dear, dear Michelle. He'd traveled a long way to find her. He was in her arms. He was home.

All he had to do was make her believe. "You are the only real thing in my life. You are what matters to me. For the rest of my life, I will protect you. I will provide for you. I will keep you safe and happy and cherished. You are my heart. Marry me. Dreams do come true."

She pressed a kiss against the pad of his thumb, damp with her tears. "Dreams end."

"Yes, they do. And that's the good part. This is the real thing." He kissed her as gently as dawn, as reverently as a man treated the most important woman on earth. "We get to live the rest of our lives together. All you have to do is say yes."

"Yes."

He pulled her into his arms, and she could feel it in the harmony that bound her heart to his, her soul to his. He was right. Their life ahead was going to be better than any dream.

"I love you," she whispered against his lips.

"Not as much as I love you." His kiss was more than a kiss. It was perfection.

Epilogue

"You've got paint on your nose." Brody laid the paintbrush on the rim of the can. His wife was looking more beautiful with every day.

Even in a secondhand T-shirt with a big hole in the shoulder, a pair of his old running shorts and speckled with blue paint, she made him brim over with tenderness.

"Hold still." He swiped the paint splatter off the bridge of her nose with the clean edge of his T-shirt. "You're getting more paint on you than on the trim."

"Oh, says the man who looks like he swam in a vat of paint." She wrapped her arms around his neck, not worried about all the dabs of blue still wet on his chest.

"Are you happy?" he asked after a long, passionate kiss.

"Hmm. Delirious."

"We're never going to get this house finished if we keep this up."

"I'm not worried about it." Her favorite place on earth was with her husband. Michelle sighed, contented, and laid her head on his chest. It was impossible to think she could be any happier than this, but she knew this was only the beginning. She knew for a fact their happiness was going to double.

A year had passed since Brody first showed up in her life. They'd had a September wedding in the church where she'd been baptized, with her family surrounding her. They'd lived in the apartment above the garage while Brody helped her dad with the harvest.

Then, after she and Brody had bought the property from her parents, they'd moved into the bungalow where Mick had stayed. Since he was in prison for a few more years, it wasn't likely he would need it.

Did she tell him now, before everybody came? Or did she wait until they were alone, the day spent, and ready to go to bed?

"What are you smiling about?" He brushed his hand down her hair with endless affection.

"I can't keep this secret any longer!" It was killing her. She thought she'd cook a nice dinner, have a romantic evening with him and then surprise him with the news.

But did she do that? No!

His eyes widened. His mouth twisted into a big smile and then he lifted her up with both hands. "You're pregnant, aren't you?"

"Yes!" She was laughing, wrapping her arms around his neck as he started whooping with joy.

"Hey, you two, keep it down, would you?" Kendra swung down from her gelding. She'd ridden over today.

Behind her Zach and Karen pulled into the driveway in their SUV. Soon Kirby and Sam would follow. Now that they had little Michael, they always ran a few minutes late.

"It's terrible, all this love in the air." Kendra winked as she untied her saddle pack. "I brought snacks."

"We brought hamburger makings," Karen added as she lifted Allie from her car seat.

Allie was clapping her hands together and singing, "Down! Down!"

Zach grabbed his tool bag. "We're here to help install those windows. C'mon, let's get started, if you can pull yourself away from your wife."

Brody pressed his forehead to hers. Michelle knew the bond between them was a precious gift. And it was only going to get better.

"I'll deal with you later," he promised.

"I hope so."

Sam and Kirby were pulling up, everyone was calling out their greetings, but it was only background noise as Michelle watched her husband amble off with Zach, talking windows and something about miter saws.

Dreams came true. Michelle knew that now. Prayers were answered. The gift of life was an amazing one, she thought, as she held out her hands to her niece as Allie came running.

A shiver skidded across the back of her neck. She turned, knowing Brody was watching her. She felt his happiness because it was hers, too. This was the good stuff in life, she had no doubt, as he whispered, ''I love you.''

As she loved him, heart and soul.

* * * * *

What will it take for Kendra McKaslin to open her heart to love? Find out in ALMOST HEAVEN by Jillian Hart, coming from Love Inspired in July 2004!

Dear Reader,

Thank you for choosing *Heart and Soul*. I am so excited to finally tell Michelle's story. I've been fond of her ever since she first appeared in my second Love Inspired story, *His Hometown Girl* (LI #180), where she was Karen's little sister. Michelle was so kind and good and waiting faithfully for the love of her life to come along. And he does, in the form of Gabe Brody, FBI, a man who is more than he seems and her answered prayer. I hope you enjoyed reading her story as much as I did writing it.

I wish you and your loved ones peace and grace.

Jillian Hart